# THE NEW MYTHIC

## A Sci-Fi and Fantasy Collection

Paddy Boylan
Alexandria Burnham
A. R. Eldridge
Matan Elul
James Healy
Phoenix Raig

Paperback ISBN: 978-0-6456614-0-8

Ebook ISBN: 978-0-6456614-1-5



Contributing authors: Paddy Boylan, Alexandria Burnham, A. R. Eldridge, Matan Elul, James Healy and Phoenix Raig.

Cover by Ajit Govett.

Contributing artwork commissions by: artguy20 ('The Traitor' and initial cover sketch) crispytheghoul ('Town Hall Steps' and 'Cooling Engines') scorpydesign ('Glyphlight') doantrang ('Enter Elias Schmidt') sohlsoli ('The Stolen Sword').

**Content warning:** This work contains graphic scenes of violence and murder.

www.precipicefiction.com

# Contents

To Jack,

Because anthologies ought to have godfathers too.

Precipice Fiction wouldn't exist without you.

# Cooling Engines

by James Healy

In the waning light, the engines throttled up and rumbled along the winding forest road. The solars powered on to light the way, but as night settled about the pines the damp autumn air turned to fog and enveloped the vehicles, trapping the light and hiding the cracks and corners in the road ahead. Their progress slowed to a crawl.

With nauseating dread, Martin watched the thickening vapour obscure the road and knew he would be held responsible.

Irate complaints grumbled down the radio, spreading across the channels in a cascade of defeat and dissatisfaction. All agreed on the same thing: the convoy would have to stop. Eighty wheels were forced to a screaming, grinding halt. Doors opened, boots scuffed on asphalt, angry voices called to one another in the dark.

From inside the nav's campervan, Martin heard the angry calls bouncing up and down the convoy's length. The barked orders. The blind accusations.

His throat tightened. A chill declared itself along his nerves.

Hot and roaring engines were switched off and left to cool, steaming in the night as they ticked, and ticked.

*The convoy is stagnant…*

His thoughts found clarity.

*… Navigators swing for less than this.*

In a delirious haze of panic, he scrambled around his trailer gathering notes and maps. Tense hands scrunched the crinkled yellowed pages in his rush. He gathered everything he needed and piled them onto the pull-out table between his bed and bathroom. Then he went to the drawer beside his bed and fetched his pistol. Making sure it was loaded, he set it on the table atop the pages.

He lit a sun-bar and positioned it with shaking, fumbling fingers. The dull beam illuminated the documents before him: how the roads cut through the rising topographies, connecting one point to the next.

*Should have considered the temperature at this altitude. Should have known there could be fog.*

The rhythm in his chest quickened.

*I've left myself culpable.*

Taking his seat, Martin began an urgent examination of the convoy's position within the mountains. Beyond his campervan the yelling voices swelled, congealing into one violent cacophony.

This was another in a line of unscheduled stops. The great steel snake would have to coil up until a way forward could be found. As navigator, this task fell to him.

Martin tried to ignore the yelling, plucking out one of the many pencils bulging from his chest pocket and focusing on the maps. He traced the lines and scanned the words, but rising from the recesses of his memory was another mist-laden night, and what the fog revealed when dawn finally came.

Fresno's trenches.

Four years.

Four years, and that night was never absent from his mind.

---

At first, none of the officers thought much of the fog rolling across the battlefield, but the enlisted soldiers under Martin's command whispered of omens. He disregarded these as fatigue and superstition. The heavy fighting was taking its toll. The enemy had tried to come across every morning now for the past two weeks and, although Martin's unit was holding the line, they were all scraped thin from the days of endless shelling and nights filled with the cries of dying men.

Each night begged the question of what horrors tomorrow would bring.

The haunting pale fog, illuminated as it was by the moon, gave their imaginations something else to fixate on. Was it dust thrown up by the explosions? Smoke from gunfire? Or a ghostly cloud descending to carry away the souls from ruined and mutilated bodies?

It was none of these. It was fog. Although not simply fog alone, but a screen, a curtain. Something in which men could go about unseen and obscured.

A man unseen has a way of behaving differently than you might expect, than you might be accustomed to in plain light. It gives way to things. Dark, lowly things.

Through the thick, eerie blanket, Martin and his unit began to hear the muted sounds of gunfire, coming from the distant trenches. Not the frantic to-and-fro of a firefight but short, unanswered bursts.

This battery was something else.

Executions.

Masked by the fog, the enemy turned to revolt, and turned their rifles on their own.

Martin and his unit waited out the night, listening to the sounds of murder die away into silence, uncertain of what it meant or how to feel about it.

The following morning, he led a squad between sinkholes and tangles of barbed wire toward the enemy lines. They passed like whispers through an empty battlefield and claimed the trenches without dispute. Most of the enemy soldiers were gone in the night. Only the loyal remained: laying stiff and cold in the dirt where they had argued and died for the cause.

But the true horror lay waiting with the officers, ambushed inside their bunkers. Stripped of command by blade and rifle butt. So gruesome were the remains that none under Martin's command could bring themselves to set foot back inside the concrete shells to remove them.

This was the insane rage of mutiny, the vindictive cruelty of the betrayer. The fuel that burned in the engine of revolt. Only this justified the act, as surely as blood and violence washed away the shame and dishonour. For the perpetrators of mutiny needed to be heroes, their victims, monsters.

Once seen this way, no punishment went too far.

Martin's soul quivered when he faced the naked and butchered bodies.

He staggered out before regaining composure, allowing his unit see the raw vulnerability, something he would never ordinarily have let happen. Commanders needed the appearance of control at all times. Remaining in that enclosed space however, with the tortured bodies, was to surely court rousing unearthly evils; Martin had no doubt such agony and malice drew the attentions of those in hell.

But try as he might, he could not unsee. The misery seared itself into his mind, no longer requiring attentive eyes. It would be with him forever.

That morning Martin understood why the Affiliation treated deserters, suspected dissidents or conspirators of mutiny, so mercilessly. They wished to make examples of them and grind underfoot any similar ideas.

This of course was exactly what bred it; betrayal begets betrayal.

---

Fresno fell. The Affiliation territory expanded. Martin left the war behind, throwing in with the roadies: rolling communities of freelancing ferrymen, transporting supplies, materials and people across the scarred and broken continent. For years Martin travelled the fractured freeways, one destination to the next, visiting everything from major colonies to squalid settlements scattered beyond the territories, but Fresno was with him everywhere, following in his tracks. It drew close now as he worked frantically over his maps.

Out there, lost to him in the dark, the passengers clamoured and yelled.

Riflemen were deployed to corral them away from the administrative vehicles. No doubt they would succeed; underfed passengers couldn't stand against armed soldiers, even if they outnumbered them four to one. But they were angry and scared, calling for answers or blood, whatever came first.

Halting would allow competing convoys to pull ahead, taking the prosperous roads and leaving only a scorched path for them to follow. Crew and passengers alike knew what scorched roads would mean. The crew would insist on diverting, possibly even abandoning the route across the border in favour of returning to the territories, but most of the passengers were destined for Eastern Settlements beyond the mountains and the spreading reach of the Affiliation.

The engines were hot and ticking. Convoys didn't sit idle in the dark like this. Not for long.

In the other vehicles, decisions were being weighed and whispered over. Everyone needed assurance. The convoy needed to stay on track.

So by the beam of the sun-bar, he poured over his maps, combing between the faded high-quality road and topographical maps from before the collapse, and the crumpled hand-scrawled drawings picked up from travelling map-makers. Martin always said a good navigator wasn't much use if he couldn't predict the changes to the landscape between when the map was printed and today—the landscape can move a lot in ten years—but neither were they any good if they couldn't spot a bluff in a mapper's illustration. Blaming the maps was virtually an admission of incompetence.

Martin could see no way forward that would take them into low enough terrain for this freezing fog to clear. Sitting idle for the night would incite the crew but backtracking now—with the border so close—would cause the passengers to erupt.

There had to be some way to keep the wheels turning, some way to cross these mountains tonight.

But this wasn't the immediate problem Martin faced. If interpreting nightmare topographies was all this post entailed, anyone could be taught to do it. No, navigation was really about steering clear of wreckage.

A convoy unexpectedly halted was a warzone, broken promises filling the air like shrapnel.

Rolling divisions averted revolt in their own manner: dousing sparks before they made flame. Too often, scarcity required these little fires be stifled with blood. Nothing else could be left on the tarmac as hastily.

At any moment now each department head would be called to a counsel before Chief Eli, to squabble over whose head was upon the block—it could be Martin's—and which direction to take next.

Advocating for the passengers, the Civics department would be clamouring about the delays, conditions and food shortages this halt would cause and insist on a speedy resolution that got the wheels turning again.

In agreement with them—although not giving a damn whether the 'short termers' were fed or not—the Mechanics department, comprised of the drivers, engineers and other crew members, would do the same. Obsessing constantly over how much fuel, battery or render was being burned, the roadies that lived long term in these convoys nevertheless could not tolerate stagnation for any period of time. Agitation and fear ran rabid amongst them at the prospect of a prolonged stop.

Every department had their own schemes and agendas—hidden behind their public posturing—and their own rear-seat dealings. Most dangerously: they were ever ready to toss blame about like a primed grenade.

And navigators made for soft targets.

Pistons would be turning, axels aligning in his direction. Martin needed to steer the blame elsewhere.

For this he required three immediate things.

First, a reason why this wasn't his fault. He could reliably divert culpability onto the drivers, given the disrepair of the roads it was impossible for them to meet time frames. They were the easiest to blame, after the navigator.

Second was a scapegoat, from each of the other departments, someone more at fault than himself. One of the speakers would certainly draw an accusation against him and he needed something loaded and chambered to use against them when they did. This would prevent the other departments from dogpiling on top of him; once they saw he was prepared to counter they wouldn't risk being called out themselves.

His third and most important requirement was a solution, a way out. This could only be a new route, a better route.

Every unit, Armament, Civics, Mechanics and Trade, would have a solution ready, a new route that served their agendas. Worst of all, one planned by their own prospective navigator. Their hopeful. Their scapegoat, their man who would plan routes that served them, until the time came to serve him up.

But they were all working in the dark. Nobody else had access to the maps. Nobody had the insight.

Because of this Martin's two personal riflemen armed themselves and set up post the instant the wheels stopped rolling. They had instructions to let nobody through—except an envoy from the Armament department, with a message from Hicks.

Martin was no scapegoat. He'd stepped to this rhythm before and with considerable eloquence. Yes, Navigation was a department of one, separate from the others so that chartering remained unbiased ... but only a fool worked in isolation.

When the council was called, Hicks, speaking for the Armament department, would claim that the convoy, halted in hostile territory, was impossible to defend. With his riflemen stirred up and angry, Hicks would insist foot patrols be sent out to scout the area. Trench lines to be dug and checkpoints set up along the road.

This claim would frighten Civics and incite the Mechanics, making the demand to push off all the more urgent and—in the midst of squabbling, posturing and conjecture about what route to take—a detailed solution all the more potent. Hicks would make this argument, motivating a pliable audience for Martin to present this new route to. Martin had a contingency and now, a plan forming too.

His pencil scratched across the old maps, trailing frantic lines, decisions, forecasts. Outside, the yells grew wilder.

Entirely absorbed, Martin didn't notice the shape climbing past the window onto the roof, nor the skylight being raised, nor even the shadow that descended through it, dropping silently to the floor.

A cold draft of night ruffled his papers.

With a jolt he glanced over his shoulder and saw the looming shadow. His hand darted for the pistol but he couldn't look away, the advancing figure was too close. Fingers probed blindly across the papers until Martin registered the younger man's face.

Eyes that peered wide and vacant from the shadows of sunken sockets. The torn flesh across his upper lip that exposed teeth in a lurid ever-present sneer.

This grisly visage was Hicks's whip, an unofficial role that involved delivering and enforcing the head of Armament's more disagreeable and unsanctioned instructions.

'God damnit, Dennis, are you trying to get yourself shot?' Martin gasped.

'Don't flatter yourself, old man,' Dennis said, staring past him at the table. 'What are you chartering?'

'What am I—' Martin's thoughts tried to catch up with his racing heart. 'What are you doing here?'

'Whispering,' Dennis hissed, 'you might try it. I'd hate to have climbed through the window for no reason.'

'Why did you climb in the window?'

Dennis frowned, 'I hope you don't leave your door unlocked as well?'

Martin curled his fingers into a fist, trying to dispel the tension constricting his nerves.

'Where's Hicks?' Martin asked, rearranging the pages to hide his work but as Dennis came forwards, Martin recoiled, leaning from the table. There was something noxious about the enforcer that dissuaded proximity.

'Trying to broker a deal.'

Martin felt cool relief breathe through him. If Hicks arranged for another department to support Martin's new route then he would be in the clear. No matter what route he suggested.

'Don't look so pleased yet, I said "trying". We're on the outside of this one.'

'How come?'

Ignoring him, Dennis scanned the table top, gaze roving from side to side.

Martin swooped across the maps, moving pages, covering lines, hiding how one connected to the other. Maps held valuable information, keenly sought after and worth guarding.

The enforcer straightened and sneered, 'What do you hear outside? Is that the rumble of fourteen engines or the bloodthirsty howls of hungry passengers? Armament is on the outs because Hicks approved this route.'

'His backing the route doesn't prove—' Martin bit down on the word. He was about to say 'collusion'.

'Prove? You're a couple miles too far outside the territories for words like that. Come on. The other units already suspect you're letting someone else plan your routes because of all the hold-ups. Now this fog? If it isn't collusion, then they'll claim you're completely incompetent.'

Martin felt the accusation flung over him like a burning blanket and rushed to get from under it.

'Nobody could have known about the fog.'

Dennis brought his narrow shoulders up to his ears in a shrug.

'Doesn't matter. You know why, don't you? Because all the other units can claim knowing about fog is exactly what your job is.' He jabbed a finger at Martin. 'You've left yourself exposed. Hicks and the whole armament department along with you.'

'I know how this works,' he said, fighting the tremble in his voice.

'So get in my lane, would you? We need a fix. Show me what you've got planned. Is there a route out of this?'

Dennis dragged the map towards himself and with it, the various paper weights. Martin watched as his pistol, placed atop the pages, scraped across the table away from him. Dennis leaned down to inspect the papers and—with a gesture that would almost have passed for absentminded if it had not been so precise—scooped up the pistol, placing it on the counter behind him.

A shiver scurried down Martin's spine.

As neatly as that, without chance for struggle or protest, he'd been disarmed.

*Hicks hasn't sent a messenger at all.*

Martin spoke with measured care, 'Why are you here?'

'I'm not here, remember. If I was here, I'd have come through the door, not down the chimney like a fuckin' Santy Clause.'

This made sense: there could be no suspicion of collusion. Hicks required a subtle hand to see his route through. Still, the enforcer was an unusual messenger.

Martin glanced again out the window. His riflemen still stood at attention, close enough to hear him yell.

He swallowed dryly and collected his thoughts.

'I mean why you and not another envoy?'

'Because people have these things called eyes, Martin,' Dennis droned, 'and these other things called mouths, that they use to spread lies ... or sometimes truth. Which is worse.'

Dennis looked up and chuckled at him. The sound was irregular and hollow.

Martin stayed silent.

Dennis's smirk melted like ice on a throttling engine. 'Listen. You rose up through Armament division and Hicks nominated you as navigator. That alone arouses suspicion. Then he was the first to support this route, I mean, you might as well tell everybody he had a hand in planning it. Now they'll be watching him—and you. We can't be seen to be conspiring. Can we?'

Martin couldn't think of any reason not to add it up like this. Dennis's reputation for delicacy bordered on superstition. Why wouldn't Hicks deploy him now, if a risky plan was in play?

'No, I suppose we can't.' Martin settled back into his chair.

Blocking the sun-bar, Dennis sat on the edge of the table, shadowing Martin.

'Now then, before the escort comes looking for you, tell me what your route is, so that I can get it to Hicks. He'll know which of the department heads will support it and he'll strike a deal with them so they'll back your route. Once you've provided a way out of here, you're out of danger. But only if Hicks can strike a deal before the meeting.'

Martin shifted uncomfortably.

He didn't like it but it made sense that this was the best way for Hicks to get the plan.

Martin stood, clearing loose papers from atop the map.

'Our options are limited,' he began.

Dennis slipped alongside him, leaning close. 'Good. Makes things simple.'

'Best way around these mountains is to the south but due to the delays they will most certainly be scorched by other convoys at this point.'

Martin didn't need to elaborate, every convoy feared following in the wake of another. Hard miles, bare blacktop, passing the ruined cities already picked through by other raiding parties, pulling into settlements and being told there was nothing they needed. Resources dwindling. Fuel, food, water and hope ebbing away.

'What about north?' Dennis asked.

'North and west of here we re-enter Affiliation territory. We can't risk that with the sun-wells showing. Affiliation patrols will halt anyone utilising alternate fuel and with the transport holds full of refugees we will look like Eastern agents.'

'So we need to find petro and strip those sun-wells off. They were a terrible suggestion. Another gift from Hicks.'

'There is no petro. The territories are dry. Why else would they have need to make laws about fuel people can and can't use? If we hadn't converted we never would have made it this far.'

'Little good if we are stranded now anyway. We should have sat tight and sourced some while we were in familiar country.'

'With these passengers? No. We needed to get out and now we need to stay clear. We aren't re-entering the territories. Let me be clear: the Eastern Settlements are still our best option. Any other direction could mean the end of this convoy.'

'Save the theatrics for the crowd, Martin. Enough of where we can't go. What's your plan?'

'We push on through these mountains at dawn. Full throttle, no breaks. Turn north at I5, get out of these mountains before nightfall and continue on for a day-and-a-half through the snow fields. That puts us back on schedule and way ahead of anyone that circumnavigated these mountains by going south.'

'Continue along this route?'

'Yes, it's the best way through. There are two small settlements in the mountains along highway sixty-four. One is a teched-out farming community that will trade crop for copper, for their sun wells. The second is a squaller but they guide people across the mountains by wagon train. Any disgruntled passengers can disembark there if they think they'll have better luck with the settlers.'

'Along this road?'

'Yes.'

Dennis turned and paced to the far end of the trailer.

Martin went on explaining his route: the precise roads they would take, which settlements they could stop at, and what could be traded at each but the farther he went the more he felt—with mounting irritation—that Dennis wasn't listening.

While Martin spoke the enforcer's gaze wandered around the camper's interior, eyeing his possessions. Some he picked up, to pry and fiddle with. First, he ogled a coffee mug like it was an alien artefact. Next, he nudged a shelf with his shoulder, wobbling and toppling Martin's assorted ornaments. Dennis watched them roll and spill to the floor, his expression unreadable. Then he plucked up a length of twine used as a belt, wrapped it around one palm and snapped it menacingly to test its strength. Finally, he gestured to Martin's wristwatch.

'You're sentimental,' he interrupted, the accusation causing Martin to lose his train of thought. He tried to recall but the derision in the enforcer's words demanded an answer.

Martin looked at his watch: a Rolex gifted by his unit, after their first deployment. Kept clean, undamaged and ticking all this time. He straightened up and nodded proudly.

'A navigator needs to remain attached to the old world. Ornaments like these ... help maintain connection.'

'You miss it.'

Dennis's grin was openly mocking.

Embarrassment washed over him at the implication. The roadies ascribed nostalgia to weakness.

'We lost so much,' he said, meeting and holding the enforcer's laughing gaze, 'most prefer not to remember because it's painful, to think about how it was. That's why so few roadies make good navigators. To understand the road ahead ... you need to keep remembering what was.'

Dennis seemed to accept this with a shrug and nodded for him to proceed.

'That's it more or less.' He just wanted it over. 'After that we descend the mountains on the northern edge of the snow fields and cross the border. We'll have the roads to ourselves and a good lead on anybody making for the Eastern Settlements.'

'That's it then?'

Martin nodded.

The silence that followed was hot and lingering.

'No good,' Dennis said with blunt finality.

Rendered speechless, Martin could only stare. This route was the best he could come up with. How was Dennis rejecting it so quickly?

The enforcer was rifling through the papers again.

'Two days hard going by solars. When will we recharge the batteries, automats, the engines?'

'They can run while the sun wells fill. I've seen other divisions travel by day, using the sun directly.'

Dennis was shaking his head.

'And at night? You expect us to what, hope scavengers and marauders find a juicier target than a halted convoy? You know we don't sit idle in the dark.'

'We'll have to travel night and day to make this route work. Put a little aside. Increase the drainage, store the excess.'

'The Mechanics will love you. Have you thought about the strain that will put on these old roadsters. The runoff yesterlight will poison the engines. The converters and charging ports will burn out running that high, anyway. No, you'll leave us stranded. What we need is petroleum. Where could we find some?'

'There's nothing, Dennis. War burned it all up. There is nowhere within miles that—'

'What could a raiding party reach,' Dennis barked suddenly, 'if they had to?'

'What? Hicks would never suggest a raid here, at night, that's too—'

'He'll go where he's told.'

Martin was struck by this insolence. Not simply because Dennis was on Hicks's leash but because Martin was too. It was Hick alone they both answered—and tattled—to.

'Where *is* Hicks?' he asked, straining to stay calm in the face of Dennis's uncoiling anger.

'He's with the Mechanics, grovelling for a deal. So stop staring at me and look at that map, you need to give them something. Where can we find more fuel?'

'It's nothing but farming settlements ahead.'

'Behind us then?'

'We aren't backtracking.' Exasperation broke Martin's tension. 'Haven't you listened to me? We can't turnabout with these passengers. We'll use the sun wells by day and store a little extra for the night. The Mechanics will have to live with that and whatever strain it puts on the engines.'

Dennis leered closer, growling. 'We can lock the transport holds and leave them along any backroad we choose. Passengers don't direct this convoy. We need to go back into familiar territory and trade something in exchange for fuel. The Affiliation's expansion has been good for us, it's been reliable. It's kept the wheels turning.'

'The Affiliation is out of petro, they are pulling back, they are about to lose this war and start to contract.'

'And before that happens we need to get east, is that it?' Dennis shook his head. 'Did Hicks concoct this whole route to ween us off petro and set up Eastern connections? Is he trying to force us into abandoning Affiliation territory for good?'

Martin clenched his fists.

'Stay the course and by the time anyone figures that out it won't matter.'

Incredulity gleamed in Dennis's sunken sockets. His grin was ghastly.

'They'll want to burn *you* for fuel.' He spoke it softly, almost sympathetically. 'Grind you up like paste and put you in the oil as thinner.'

'Let me present my route, I can get the other departments on board.' Anger steadied his voice. 'It's all about how you sell it, Dennis, let me sell it.'

Dennis sighed and looked to the ceiling. Up there amidst the light fixtures and solar tubing he seemed to reach a decision. When he levelled his attention on Martin again his words were pointed and definite, his eyes snarling.

'We aren't going any further down this road. Scouts radioed in. Roads impassable.'

Martin's innards tightened as though being wrung.

He'd been afraid of a block on these quiet forest roads. Was it an abandoned crash? A fallen tree? A tree would be worse, where there was one there could easily be more, leading to halt after halt.

*Oh Christ, why didn't he mention this before?*

This could be bad for him.

'Okay,' he exhaled the word slowly, trying to think, 'this is just a holdup. We can move it. It's only trees.'

'Roads deadlocked, Martin,' Dennis spat. 'Sell that.'

Horror strangled a gasp out of Martin.

It was the death sign of a route. An abandoned stretch of gridlocked vehicles, weathered to rust, overgrown and picked clean by animals and scavengers, impossible to clear.

It spelt the dead end to his charted route and Hicks's eastbound plan.

'How? How is there a deadlock this far out? There's nothing here.' Dizzy and weak, he sank into his chair.

*We're turning about. No avoiding it.*

There was no way to pass this off to someone else now. He was at the mob's mercy.

Out there in the woods the clamouring protests reached a wailing savagery, all but drowning out the barked orders for calm.

*I'm doomed. They'll hang me for this.*

Dennis twisted the map around so Martin could see it and began tracing his finger along the road.

'Despite the fog our brave scouts travelled further down the road' He jabbed a finger down. 'They got this far. That's where it starts. To their credit they got out and walked for a stretch.' Dennis glowered at him. 'Nothing but bumpers.'

Martin wasn't listening. He was sinking into a stupefied daze.

*There shouldn't be a deadlock in such a deserted place. There's no reason for it.*

Then Dennis's words sank in.

With them, a sting of hope.

He looked up, eyeing the enforcer.

*How could he know this? The scouts didn't broadcast on open channels, only direct to the chief on a closed-circuit radio. Chief Eli wouldn't share this with Hicks.*

Martin straightened, rising out of the chair. 'How did you hear?' Grasping at the straws, he asked, 'Hicks's man in the scouting cars?'

Martin knew Hicks didn't have anyone riding in the orbiting vehicles—but if Dennis didn't, he might take the worm.

Dennis's mouth turned up in a true sneer. Finally, the grotesque and mangled lip fit the face.

'No, Martin, I got it from Chief Eli.'

Martin swallowed dryly, trying to comprehend the angle of the corner he was hurtling into. Why would Eli tell Armament before the other departments?

'Has Hicks worked something out with the chief?'

'Hicks doesn't know yet. I heard it from Eli directly.'

There was a sensation of falling.

Martin's survival to date was predicated upon anticipating the bumps and swerves in the road ahead. This lunged out of the back seat and caught him by the throat.

'But you're Hicks's man?' he stuttered, wondering where—if anywhere—Dennis's loyalties lay.

Dennis's expression flared with an anger that made Martin back away and trip into his chair.

'I'm nobody's fuckin man.' Spit flew from the mutilated mouth. 'Not Hicks's or any of the other department heads. They all might think I am but that's because the chief wants them to think that way.'

Realisation smashed down on Martin like a collapsed roof. Dennis was a rogue, unmarried to any department.

'You play one unit against the other.'

'On the contrary: I'm the eternal harmoniser. I'm the only thing keeping them from anarchy. I'm the one who keeps the wheels turning and resources flowing in. I maintain order. I make sure none of the units gouge each other's eyes out. And that the soldiers don't turn their guns on the passengers. And that the passengers don't strangle us in our beds. I'm the reason we don't starve to death sitting in a fucking halting pattern or at the side of some empty stretch of road because we ran out of fuel.' He spat this out like uncooked meat. 'You don't know why there's a deadlock up there? Well then maybe we need a navigator that does.'

'Jesus, what is this? Am I being thrown under?'

Dennis leaned back against the counter, unspooling the twine belt from his hand.

'A deal is being brokered,' he said, dangling the twine and twirling it in the air. 'Hicks may not know he's brokering it, but he will very shortly.'

'And what about me?'

Dennis levelled a finger at him. 'You'll take full blame for this. You'll have to.'

*That's it, I'm being thrown out like spent cartridges.*

'Why didn't you tell me this from the start? Was that always the plan or have you decided it in the last couple of seconds?'

Dennis didn't look at him. His gaze was fixed intently on the twine chord, coiling it round and around his palm.

'I wanted your route,' he said with an amused shrug. 'You're a navigator, Martin, you have your maps to see what roads we can take. I do something similar. I needed your plan to know what options we had.'

'And they are?'

Turning his attention to the ceiling, Dennis went on with the air of someone thinking aloud.

'Hicks will lead a night raid out in search of petro because he's responsible for you. You're his man and he needs to make amends, win back some good faith from the chief ... he'll stay out until he finds us something to run the engines with.'

'How will they know I'm his man? Are you going to tell them?'

'No. You are,' Dennis snapped, 'right now, here. You'll write it.'

He grabbed the pencils and handful of charcoal from Martin's pocket and slapped them down on the map before them.

Martin recoiled. 'Expose our own conspiracy? You can't be serious?'

Dennis ignored him. 'You'll say "I'm sorry, Hicks, but I can't betray the convoy. This is the best route". And you'll mark out a new route. Leading us north, back into Affiliation territory.'

'They'll lynch him.'

Dennis shook his head. 'The admin would never let it out. If anyone learnt the extent to which we manipulate our routes, letting one settlement prosper and another starve based on personal interests,' he chuckled absurdly, 'how would we look?'

Martin's heart thundered. His pulse ran in his ears.

'So this is your way of protecting the convoy? Salvaging our reputation?'

'This is your way of salvaging your life. Are you listening to what's happening out there? They're baying for someone's blood. Your blood, because the deadlock is *your* fuck up. We will have to turn about, you understand? When that gets out, the passengers will tear you apart.'

Dennis didn't need to elaborate on that.

For a moment Martin was back on his knees crawling out of the bunker in Fresno. Nausea swirled and his knees went numb.

'It has to play out like a completely new route, not a reaction to a dead end.'

'And how does it play out for me if I do this?'

'Admit to being Hicks's pawn and manipulating the route. It'll bloody his nose, but nobody will move against him for it. They've all got pawns and schemes of their own. Set a precedent like that and it's hard to argue against the same serving when it's your turn. They'll keep it covered. You'll be let out quietly.'

'And the mob?'

'You'll be forgotten.' Dennis waved a hand. 'They'll accept a change of navigator as change for the better. Maybe someone from Civics, that will really play well. Might even sell the turn-about as their idea.'

'I feel sick, like my guts are all knotted up.'

Ignoring him Dennis pressed on, 'Take this pencil and write yourself out of a skinning, would you.'

Martin took the pencil from him and looked down at the maps, following the roads backwards.

'Hicks will kill me for betraying his route, he's got forty soldiers under his command. Rabid to be let off the leash.'

'They'll all kill you if you don't do it. We're on the verge of mutiny here. Once that deadlock is announced the other heads will want you swinging from the side of a trailer. To appease the mob but also to get their own man in here, you understand? And the chief will green light it, to quieten everything down. He'll probably tie you to the grill of his own RV. Make a bauble of you. You ever seen that, touring with your daylight divisions? I doubt it. Not so pretty a thing in the light.'

Martin hadn't, but he'd heard the cries of people mounted on hoods and roofs before throttling engines mercifully covered their unanswered pleas.

They had done so with his predecessor, before Martin took the post.

Martin shut his eyes trying to block out the memory.

*'Nothing like that would happen to you, Martin,' Hicks assured him when they discussed his being nominated. 'Only the careless get caught between the spokes like that ... you're no scapegoat.'*

'So you know, then ...' Dennis' words were caustic silk, '... the kind of trouble we're facing? We are all in the firing line if this spins out. It's every man for himself now, Martin, and you are the man to stand behind.'

He was right. Martin knew he was right. A deadlock spelt death for any navigator, there was no fooling himself. He just couldn't reason how there was one here.

*Was it just bad luck, like the fog, or could I have known?*

His chest compressed, the weight of his failure crushing the air from him.

'This is your best shot. I'm not saying that to help you. It's not why I'm here, I'm here to stop this boiling over. You do this and you survive tonight, then however many more you need to until you can disembark. Mix in with the passengers until then, lay low. I don't really care. We are running out of time, so fucking write it.'

Martin nodded, feeling the energy drain from him—burnt off through fear. Unable to argue further he sank into the corner and scrawled a new route across the map with Dennis leering over him the whole time, instructing and correcting, reminding him of the urgency.

'This is a very shaky wagon we are riding, you understand that, don't you? A lot of moving parts, Martin, always working their way loose if we don't keep them fed and babied and scared into staying in place.'

The sound of his voice grated. The working of his torn lips and the ceaselessly darting gaze. By the time he finished writing, Martin was desperate to be anywhere but in the presence of Dennis.

He looked down at the note and all it contained. *This is mutiny. I am deserting my post and this note is a coup-de-grace for my officer: a surprise stab in the back.*

Something ruptured inside, bleeding shame.

'I can't do this.'

'Course you can.'

'I am an officer. An officer doesn't abandon his duty like this. You would know that if you were any kind of soldier, Dennis.'

Martin tossed the pencil to the table. It rolled across the papers and bounced into the darkness.

Dennis's gaze didn't follow, it held steady and distant. The impression reminded Martin of a reptile's cold-blooded, abiding stillness.

Dennis's hand darted out, viper swift, and snatched the note from between Martin's hands. Dennis backed off, beyond reach.

Martin was on his feet in an instant.

'Give it back.'

Drive shafts spun, ignitors sparked. Martin saw it flat and objective, from the outside in.

*Everyone's head in a different noose but only one needs to fall.*

The fog cleared and the terrain lay naked and open before him.

*They don't need an admission, they don't even need guilt.*

'I won't be the fall guy. I won't betray Hicks.'

Dennis didn't reply. In the sun-bar's light, his sockets were black pits. Down at his waist, just beyond the torchlight, Dennis held the twine belt, ends wrapped around his hands.

Martin didn't pursue, instead he edged towards the counters remembering something Dennis hadn't. He glanced down at his pistol, forgotten and unguarded. Martin turned, reaching for it, feeling control slip back into his fingers.

He didn't feel Dennis advance until he was at his back. The enforcer barrelled into him from behind, knocking him into the counter and pinning him against its top.

They both scrambled for the gun. Flailing gestures, grasping fingers. A tangle of limbs, interlocked and reaching. Their struggling knocked the gun farther out of reach. Martin drew his elbows to his chest meaning to push off the counter, driving Dennis back and away from the pistol but something was pulling at his hands, drawing them together, burning his skin. The twine belt was running between his wrists, Dennis had looped his hands while they fought for the gun.

Martin felt a knee press into his back. Both hands were yanked up to his shoulder. The belt snaked about his neck. Again it tightened.

He was knotted up before he could grasp what was happening.

Twine bit the soft skin of his neck, squeezing his windpipe.

He tried to speak but only splintered rasps broke free.

He was pulled from the counter, his legs kicked from beneath him. He fell to his knees. He tried to pull away.

A knee struck the back of his head and he toppled forwards.

He landed painfully on his elbows. Weight landed down on his back. Dennis was sitting on him. He felt the belt going taut as Dennis leaned back, pulling.

The Rolex shattered, coming away in pieces across the floor.

Panic screamed in Martin's head. His body contorted.

His legs ground across the carpeted floor for purchase but only kicked uselessly and toppled chair. He tightened the muscles in his neck and struggled but his arms were bound tight and pinned beneath him. He tried to roll but each time he moved Dennis repositioned swiftly, pulling in the opposite direction.

A fire burnt in his chest.

*There has to be a way out of this*, he thought.

Then his vision narrowed. A deep blackness crowded in from the edges.

*There has to be a way ...*

When the navigator's desperate fidgeting came to a stop, Dennis uncoiled the twine, rolled the body over and heaved it into a sitting position.

Here he paused to catch his breath, ensure that the sentries were still at a distance and shook some of the pain from his hands. Twine did not make for an easy garotte.

Moving quickly, he ran the belt through the ceiling fixtures and knotted it in place. One end he looped into a noose. He positioned the chair beneath. Taking the body under the arm and letting the chest fall over his shoulder, Dennis hoisted it onto himself, took a deep breath and stepped up onto the chair. Working by feel he looped the noose around the neck and stepped back.

The ceiling fixtures groaned but held the swaying corpse. They might go soon but the effect would be accomplished.

He surveyed the scene: the scattered papers and toppled ornaments. All looked well. A few adjustments were made—he tipped-over the chair, cleaned up the pieces of Rolex, rolled down the navigator's sleeves—then Dennis slipped out of the camper as quietly as he'd entered, replaced the skylight and vanished into the fog leaving only the navigator's body and suicide note behind.

By the time word got out about the deadlock, Martin's body had been discovered, his suicide note presented before the council and then destroyed, night patrols sent out to comb the area for threats and resources, and the convoy was ready to proceed with a new route, presented by a new navigator.

For another night calamity had been outpaced. Passengers and crew alike lay their heads down to the sound of order, direction and calm.

The ticking of engines silenced.

Tomorrow they would throttle along a new route, past different terrain, and under fresh direction, but always in the same manner—and as always, they would need cooling down again.

# GLYPHLIGHT

by Matan Elul

They are looking for their father.

Danica and her brother discover the corpse deep within the mine, as they step out of the lower lifts. The Glyphlight is gone, and Danica had never seen a dead man before. The mouth of the corpse is slacked open, the face covered in ash. Her attention is immediately drawn to the eyes. They're engorged, and swollen, and rise from their sockets like a pair of overripe grapes. Their watery shine makes her stomach turn.

The man is not their father.

Danica thinks that the manner in which the dead man lies is peculiar. His arms are crossed, his palms flat on his shoulders. Her older brother Mikhail tells her the man is Bojan, and that his eyes were sick with Dweller's Rot. That Bojan had worked with Father, that the lifts would take them no further and that the rest of the way can only be taken afoot. But the tunnel ahead is dark, spotted with glistening lodes of ore that infest the rock like little cancers inside a dying throat. When Danica raises her lamp, she thinks about the black heart of the Myshkin Mine, and imagines Bojan and his rotten eyes, only now he is not lying down, but standing just beyond the light of her lamp, waiting for her and Mikhail to proceed.

Danica tries to turn back towards the lift.

Mikhail blocks her path. 'Where are you going?'

'Misha.' She clutches his arm. 'It's so dark in here.'

'We have a lamp.'

'Mother said that the Glyphlight keeps the miners safe.'

'Mother also said not to go looking for Father. Do you want to leave him here over a superstition?'

'No, but—'

'There are four junctions ahead. Each leads to a new set of crosscuts, deeper into the mine. Father works down in the third, with the other veteran miners. Bojan should have been there too. If Father was there when the blackout happened, he would have stayed put.'

'How will we find him in the dark?'

'We won't.' Mikhail smiles and gestures at their bowl-shaped lamp, hotly burning through its little kerosene tank. 'He will find us.'

He is just fourteen. But boys go to the mines even younger. Danica, twelve, has never been allowed deeper than the lifts go. The Underearth is foreign to her. Uncomfortable. Her posture is spooked, her fingers clasped around the aluminium handle.

'Give me the lamp.'

'What?'

'I'll go alone,' Mikhail says. 'There's nothing to worry about, Dani.'

'You can't.'

'And besides, look at you. You're frightened out of your skin. I shouldn't have brought you here in the first place. Just go home.'

She wants to argue. She wants to show him that she isn't frightened. That she is just as desperate to find Father as he is. But rather than speak, or move, she is lost in her own dark thoughts about the dark depths ahead, imagining all that could linger in the absent light.

All this time the two of them have not moved an inch from the lifts that have lowered them into the Myshkin Mine depths. Now, impatient, Mikhail takes the lamp from her hands and ushers her away.

'Go home,' he mouths confidently, 'I'll see you soon.'

Danica hears a sound. A heavy, sinewy-swift scuttle from the distant darkness. She is not afraid. Not at first. The sound is so unexpected, so *alien*, that she cannot decide if what she heard was real.

She feels as if she had been meant to scream, but had missed her cue.

Meanwhile, Mikhail advances.

She hears the sound again. A sort of slither. Picking up speed. Then, incredulously hesitant. As if something was moving—stopping—rushing—stopping—rushing.

Gone, again.

'There's something,' she finally whispers. 'I heard it.'

'What?' Mikhail stops. 'Are you sure? Where is it?'

'Somewhere near.'

'Can you see it?'

Danica shakes her head. 'We should go back,' she whispers, and her voice sounds childish to her, and unreasonable. 'Please.'

Mikhail waits for a long moment. He surveys the darkness around him. He looks from Danica to the path ahead. He listens, quietly, alertly. He doesn't move until a whole minute of such silence passes, and then after another, he turns slowly to his sister and asks again, 'Are you sure?'

'Yes!'

The darkness around Mikhail feels suddenly thick with presence. Danica remembers visiting the mine when the Glyphlight still shined. The light had been as bright as the mid-summer morning, like oxygen flushing the veins of the Myshkin Mine.

Now it is all black.

*The light is a wall, Dani,* her father once told her. *Make sure you stay on the right side of it.*

When her brother looks at her, she feels the weight of his indecision in his grim expression. He seems torn between wanting to believe her and accepting the consequences. If you are lying now, about something like this, he must think, how can I ever believe you again? But if she isn't lying, if Mikhail chooses to believe her, won't that mean doing the unthinkable and leaving their father behind?

It was Mikhail's idea to come here. When Father hadn't come home during the night, nor the morning that followed. Mother argued against it. She made them promise that they would not go. Standing awkwardly stiff in front of her sickbed, the two siblings told her what she wanted to hear.

Danica had doubled the amarantus in Mother's tea. When the sun had set, they went to the mine.

And now, hours later, Mikhail is standing between Danica and the darkness, and decides there is nothing there.

He whispers, less than whispers, 'There's nothing here.'

'*Misha*,' she half gasps. 'Misha, please come back.'

He goes ahead into the mine. Lamp in hand.

She considers, again, and again and again, that her brother is right. That whatever she had heard had been imagined. That the fright crawling inside her is the product of her own mind, and not of anything else. Absentmindedly, she follows her older brother into the darkness.

He walks fast, angry.

Danica doesn't know whether to argue her point or apologise for wanting to leave their father behind. She thinks, suddenly, what a bad daughter she must be. What shame would swell inside her when they find their father, injured or hurt or lost inside the Myshkin Mine. Would Mikhail tell him? Would he tell Father, *your daughter wanted to leave you here?* That she was spooked by the dark?

But when she fancies her father's face, all she can see is the image of Bojan's pale face and his swollen dark eyes. The sight of it comes fast, and fiercely blazes inside her mind. She sees it as clearly as she sees her brother's silhouette up ahead, and a cold panic flushes through her.

She lets out a sob.

She feels Mikhail's arms around her. She looks up, and her older brother is there, already returned. He is not angry anymore. 'Go back,' he says gently. 'I'll look for him by myself.'

But she cannot hear him. She cannot listen. She looks left, and right, and left, and right, searching for the hollowed face she had seen. For the black bursting eyes and the slacked jaw. Her brother tightens his embrace, and then he gently goads her towards the lifts. Mikhail says something about the glyphlight. Glorified lamps. He says that there is nothing down here. Except for Father.

She wants desperately to believe.

But beyond the glare of the lamp, the shadow twists into the bent light, floating like dark eels. Meanwhile, her brother prepares her to leave. Ushers her to the door of the lifts. Does he not see the delighted darkness behind them? Does he not feel the eager dread?

Danica knows at this point that the darkness is not a trick of the mind. That the noise she had heard had been real. And now, she hears it again. Right behind her shoulder. Close enough that she can feel it in the air.

The fear that takes hold of her at that moment is so real, so possessive, that she half turns to enter the lifts, about to leave her brother behind.

The sound is different now. No more scuttling. No more slithering. She hears it, and it is laughing, laughing and screaming and sobbing and *pounding* the earth with legs, celebrating maniacally the arrival of the boy marching into the darkness.

Closer, closer, closer.

She is inside the lift now. Her cold numb fingers touch the sleek iron lever. Mikhail is outside, still smiling, still reassuring. She looks past him, at the dancing shadows, at the dimly lit mouth of the tunnel, and her mouth slacks open with shock.

Bojan's corpse is gone.

Danica has to be fast. She leaps out of the lift, moving like a possessed, single-minded wraith, and then she tears the lamp from her brother's hand and tosses it over her head and into the distant darkness. Mikhail lunges after it, but he cannot hope to reach it, and the two of them are locked limb to limb when the blazing light plummets ahead, swallowed by the darkness without even the slightest indication of broken glass.

This was their only way to navigate this mine.

She cannot see her brother anymore, and she is thankful because she cannot imagine facing the betrayal that must be burnt across his face.

---

It is morning. The Glyphsmith doesn't come.

They tell the rest of the villagers what has happened in the mine. The mayor gathers a group of men with kerosene lamps and pistols. Mikhail is not permitted to join them. The siblings wait outside the mine in the freezing cold for any sign of the group's return. The night passes. Another contingent of village militia enters the mine at dawn. They carry rifles. The siblings are sent home. Danica walks with a hollow stomach and Mikhail straggles behind her.

He keeps his distance.

Their house is surrounded by blood-red sycamores. The red leaves scatter on the crumbled roof tiles, and pile on the rotten awning. The door is faded, full of scratch marks. Danica has lost sight of Mikhail. She does not know where he went, nor when he will return.

She enters the house and finds her mother in bed.

Mother's thin eyelashes flutter when she senses Danica. She sits up and places her slender hands on her lap. Her gaunt cheeks burrow into her jaw. When she speaks, her voice is fragile and weightless. 'You went to look for your father.'

Danica nods.

There is no anger in her mother. Danica wonders if Mother had been relieved to discover her children had gone looking for their father. When her gaze crosses with her mother's for the first time, there is silence. Danica is shaking with shame. She waits for her mother to ask about Mikhail, or Father.

There is much to be said, but neither speaks. Danica stares at her bedridden mother and a sadness fills her. She suddenly wonders if she is strong enough to help Mother down the stairs, the way Father had.

Danica hears the hungry whines of Beris from the bottom floor. Soon his cries will wake five-year-old Sasha too. Opposite her, Mother tries and fails to rise from her bed. Her sickness has spread from beneath her white blouse to the pale flesh of her neck. The veins on her throat are black and bold. They throb when she breathes.

Beris's cries intensify and Mother flinches as if someone has stomped on her toe.

Mother struggles for a moment. Later Danica will tell her what she has seen inside the mine. That men with guns went to look for Father inside the Myshkin Mine, and that Mikhail will return soon. That the Glyphlight is gone.

But all these things can wait. For now, Danica descends the stairs, goes to the kitchen and pours a cup of old oats into the saucepan atop the stove.

Her little sister Sasha has already been woken by Beris's tantrum. She, too, is hungry.

---

The mine foreman arrives at the house the following week to settle Father's account. His final wages are twenty-six pence silver and ninepence bronze. Mother thanks him with a fragile smile. He glares at the dark veins on her throat. He says nothing, and leaves quickly.

The money lasts them two weeks.

With the mine shut until further notice, most of the Myshkin men now seek work in Gulam. The city is far, and the glyphtrain circumvents the village by thirteen miles, so most of the work seekers do not return home on a daily basis. They send money to their families with relatives and friends or try to make a weekly visit.

Those families whose men have not returned from the mine are less fortunate.

Mikhail goes with them. On his first visit home, he is wearing grey overalls and his left eye is purple and swollen like a plum. He gives Mother sixpence silver and twopence bronze, and she immediately sends Danica to the grocer for some much-needed flour and salt. The next time Mikhail returns from Gulam he only has fourpence silver, and the look in his eyes keeps Danica awake for hours during the night.

The money is barely enough for food, let alone medicine for Mother, whose skin is getting paler, and veins darker. The apothecary is a nice, pot-bellied man with bright red cheeks. When Danica comes to his shop, twelve-bits shy of the twopence price tag of the amarantus root she needs for Mother's salve, the apothecary asks Danica if she is good at cleaning.

She says that she is.

He gives her the key to his shop that night. She mops the floor, wipes clean the stone bannisters and scrubs the dirty, chemical-filled basin until it is spotless. After that, she polishes the empty vials, scours the saucepans shiny and rinses all the towels, clothes and brushes that the apothecary has used. She also hears what she thinks is the squeak of a birch mouse from behind a large cabinet.

She does not clean there.

Once, in the night, she thinks she sees the silhouette of a man just outside the shop. When she looks out the window, she does not recognise his face. He is wearing a thick winter cloak, even though Myshkin is quite hot this time of the year.

The man stands beneath a lamplight for a few minutes and then leaves, but Danica remains by the window a while longer.

The apothecary returns in the morning and stares at her quietly for a long time. He tells her that she wasn't meant to stay here the whole night and clean so thoroughly. That he had only meant for her to mop the floor. Awkwardly, she apologises. The man says he does not have money to pay her, that times are hard, and that it is inappropriate of her to assume such a job without requisition.

She promises that the amarantus root is payment enough. The next evening, she comes to the apothecary again and asks if he needs the shop cleaned.

He politely refuses.

One night Mikhail says that he has heard rumours about the mine. 'They're going to open it,' he says between spoonfuls of watery cabbage soup. 'Ingar said things are becoming insufferable, and that the mayor told the duke, and that the duke sent a firm letter to the king.'

'Don't believe everything Ingar says,' Mother replies. This is one of her better days. She is sitting downstairs, her pale skin just a touch more pink than usual. Beris is sitting in her lap, pointing his wooden spoon at Danica, who is sitting opposite them.

'You know he likes to talk,' Mother continues.

'He says,' Mikhail continues, 'that the king said he'll send one of his *absolvers.*'

'Nonsense,' Mother says. 'Absolvers aren't real.'

'They are,' Mikhail answers hotly. 'And one of them is coming to the village to deal with our problem.'

'What problem?' Sasha pushes her still-full bowl away from herself.

'Finish your soup,' Mother says.

'No!' Sasha exclaims and turns to her older brother expectantly.

'Absolvers are devil hunters,' Mikhail says. 'And the problem is that we have a real big devil living in the village mine.'

'Devil?' Sasha's eyes widen.

'*Misha—*'

Mikhail ignores his mother. 'Yes, the devil that killed Father.'

'Mikhail!' Mother cries out, and her pale face is flustered with exertion.

Mikhail leans closer to Sasha and looks her in the eyes. 'You see, it was waiting for Father to go to work, and when he did it jumped on him and snapped him right in half—'

*Thwack!*

Mother slaps Mikhail hard on the cheek and immediately she bursts into a raspy fit of coughing. Beris starts crying and Sasha tears up too. Through it all, Mikhail remains in his seat, stunned for a moment, before erupting out of his chair and stomping away from the dinner table. His eyes are glistening with hurt, but he says nothing.

Danica pats her mother on the back and draws little Beris from her arms. 'It's okay, little Beri-bear,' she coos to her baby brother. His sobbing softens, and she cradles him in her arms, rocking him back and forth until he is calm.

Mother continues coughing. The black veins on her throat have reached the bottom of her chin. Danica hates them. They remind her of little black worms, wriggling through the earth. She watches them sometimes, wishing desperately that they would stop their excruciating crawl. Some of the veins climb up Mother's nape, hiding beneath the scant remains of her hair.

Soon they would reach her brain.

Later, after Mother returned to her bed, Beris put in his crib and Sasha tucked into the straw bed beside him, Danica finds Mikhail downstairs sipping from a bottle of gakkul small enough to pocket.

'Is that why you've been bringing less wages?' Danica asks. 'Because you're buying alcohol?'

'That's none of your business.'

'Father wouldn't want you to drink this stuff.'

'Father?' Mikhail asks. 'The one you made me leave behind in that mine to die? The one you betrayed?'

Danica flushes but she stands her ground. Mikhail has changed much since he started going to Gulam for work. It's not only the alcohol. He is stealing cigarettes from his co-workers at the factory. She washes his clothes, and the smell of smoke sticks to them like feathers to tar.

When she sits down beside him, he stirs uncomfortably.

She stays quiet. The two of them are alone in the living room. Danica stares ahead into the dark window and Mikhail clutches his bottle but doesn't drink.

'I hate this,' Mikhail says without looking at her. 'I fucking hate all of this. I hate the mine. I hate Myshkin. I hate Gulam, and those stupid people at the stupid factory. They're the worst sort of bastards.'

She nods.

'It's just ... it's just.' Mikhail looks down and pauses. When he speaks next, his voice cracks into pieces. 'Mother *shouldn't hit me.*'

'I know.'

She pulls him into her arms and he falls quietly apart. Danica embraces him. When he retreats from her, wiping his eyes with strange, almost forgetful indifference, Danica too acts as if the moment had not occurred.

The silence that follows is not unpleasant. Mikhail puts the bottle on the table.

'It's real, you know,' Mikhail says. 'What Ingar said.'

'About the king sending an Absolver to fix everything?' Danica asks.

'Yes.'

'I believe you,' Danica replies.

'You do?' Mikhail looks incredulous. 'Why?'

'I just do,' she says, and after a moment adds. 'And I think I've seen him.'

'You saw the Absolver? How did you know that it was him?'

'I didn't know his face,' Danica explains. 'And he was wearing a dark travel cloak. Only outsiders wear cloaks to Myshkin this time of year. He is probably regretting that decision. So, I suppose that must be your Absolver.'

'I guess it could be.'

'Why else would an outsider come here?' Danica smiles gently.

'Hah!' Mikhail turns in his seat wearing a big fat grin. He looks happier than Danica has seen him in months. 'I knew it! So how come you've seen this guy so much?'

Danica hesitates. She is not certain what she should say. Eventually, beneath the glow of her brother's first smile in a long time, she caves. 'This Absolver of yours has been here for weeks, Mikhail. In fact, I think he's been following me.'

'Following *you*? Why?'

'I'm not sure.'

'Well.' Mikhail scratches his head and nods. 'I think it's time we find out.'

Mr Oraculi is crushingly drunk when the siblings find him at the *Ragged Stoat.* He is more shroud than a man, wrapped in a thick traveller's cloak. He tilts up and down in his seat, gripping a tankard so hard that his knuckles are white with strain. There is a strong odour about him. When he spots Danica and Mikhail, he smiles wide and waves them over.

'Y'finally came!' He exclaims. '*Mistah Oraculi*, at your services.'

The siblings hesitate. The man continues to gesture them to his table.

'Are you an Absolver?' Mikhail asks flatly, after coming closer. 'Crypts, what have you been drinking? It smells like the guts of a weasel here.'

'Oh, y'know, a bit of *this* and a whole lot of *that*,' Mr Oraculi says. He looks at them with a silly and satisfied look on his face. 'It's a pleasure, really.'

'Are you really an Absolver?' Danica repeats her brother's question.

'I s'pose I am!' Mr Orcauli says. 'But you already knew that much, din't ya?'

'Have you been following my sister?'

'Yes, I have.'

'Why?' Danica is taken aback by the frankness. 'What do you want from me?'

'You, uh, how do I, uh...' Mr Oraculi leans in closer and gestures at Mikhail to do the same before whispering, rather loudly, 'How do I put this in a manner that doesn't sound ... *awful*?'

'You choose your words carefully,' replies Mikhail.

'Uh, well, y'see ... Yer sister is special.'

'Special?' Danica asks.

'I've heard all about you!' Mr Oraculi nods eagerly. 'Everybody in town is talking about it. About how ye went looking for your father—both brave and insane—and how you ... you ran out.'

Mikhail looks down. Danica looks at him, at first uncertain at his reaction and then, slowly, realising. Not the story of how *they* ran out. Not the story of how *they* left their father in the mine.

Only her.

She feels her gut tighten. How many times had Mikhail said that story? And to how many people?

Mikhail doesn't look at her when she says, slowly, 'Why does that make me special?'

'You ran away!' The drunk Absolver wobbles up from his chair. 'No one else did. You see, every single person that went down that mine went as deep as they could. And they were cautious, trust me, I've seen them with their rifles and their torches and their numbers. But it didn't matter. Know why?'

The siblings shake their heads.

The Absolver leans closer and taps the side of his head. 'Because of their *ears.*'

Danica begins to understand. 'They couldn't hear it.'

'Exactly!'

'Hear what?' Mikhail asks.

'He couldn't hear it either, could he? At least that's what he's been telling around town.' The Absolver rounds the table excitedly until he is right beside Danica. 'But you, you could?'

'Hear *what*?' Mikhail repeats.

Danica looks down. The memories of the mine flood her brain and her heart quickens in her breast. She stares at this eccentric man who seems to understand exactly what happened to her on that night, and finds herself more unnerved than relieved.

'These people who went down the mine,' Mr Oraculi says, 'they saw nothing, they heard nothing, they found nothing—until the *nothing* found them! Don't be humble! Say it! Say it, little Danica! What made you flee that rotting piece of hell? What made you *run*?'

Her blood runs hot through her face. The answer is heavy on her lips. 'Because I heard it come.'

'Ding-ding-ding!' Mr Oraculi rings an invisible bell. 'You *heard it*! You heard the demon! You heard it stalking up the slope and you did what every person with a half ounce of brain inside their little skull would do! You fled!' He turns suddenly to Mikhail. 'Did *you* hear it, young man?'

Mikhail hesitates. 'No.'

'Exactly!' Mr Oraculi exclaims. 'Neither did the other seventeen poor buggers who went into that crypt.' After a pause that seems almost too contemplative for his drunken state he says, 'Neither did your father.'

There is something odd about the Absolver. A dark weight in his eyes. When he speaks again, he does not feel drunk to Danica. He feels, in fact, like the echoed whistle at the bottom of a black chasm, calling out to the wanderers on the mountain slope.

He says, very slowly, tempestuously, '*Unless ...*'

Danica stiffens. So does her brother. She can hear the breath hitch in her brother's throat and knows her own breath is similarly sieged.

'Unless what?' They ask in unison.

'These things, these *matters* are often rather hereditary,' Mr Oraculi replies. 'It is not out of the question that if little Danica here can *hear* those dark-dwelling creatures, then so can your father.'

Danica is stunned. 'Are you saying our father is—'

'It's been months,' Mikhail interrupts her. 'Of course he isn't.'

'No,' Mr Oraculi agrees. 'Probably not.'

Probably. The word sneaks into Danica's ears and carves itself a bloody spot inside her brain. Of course Father couldn't have survived inside the mine for more than three months on his own. Even if he could elude the thing that killed Bojan and the others, what would he eat? What would he drink?

*He could have made it to the underground storerooms,* a tiny voice inside Danica urged. *They have tins there, and barrels of oil and gakkul.*

Even so, why wouldn't Father come out then?

*Because it isn't safe.*

'Assuming we believe all of this,' Mikhail says with thick scepticism in his tone, 'you've still left one key detail unexplained.'

'Oh, what is it?' The Absolver asks innocuously.

'Isn't it your goddamn job to go down that mine and *deal* with this creature?'

Mr Oraculi stares thoughtfully into one of the empty tankards. 'Yes, that is what I've been sent here to do.'

'And?' Mikhail prods impatiently. 'Why haven't you already?'

'My ears,' Mr Oraculi admits with a sad frown. 'I've tried other methods of course. But the Hassar—demon as you might call it—that settled down there, is rather *prepared* for the methods I've got in my employ.'

'So, you, you what,' Mikhail is flustered with anger. 'You quit?'

'Of course!' Mr Oraculi exclaims. 'Wouldn't you?'

'But it's your job!'

'Buggers and bolts, it is!' Mr Oraculi says. 'Don't you think I want to do it? I'd love to! There's two thousand silverpence in it for me. I'd be running down that mine yesterday if I could!' He once again gestures at his ears and sighs, as if stating the obvious. 'Nothing. I'll be just another fish in this miserable barrel, going down there.'

Strange, Danica thinks, that an Absolver cannot hear or see the creature. Are Absolvers not the specialists trained in slaying them? An idea forms in her mind.

'What if I come with you?'

Mikhail is shocked. 'Have you lost your senses, Dani?'

'You would do that?' Mr Oraculi looks elated. 'You would come down there with me?'

'She will not!'

She stares down at the table. Mr Oraculi tentatively raises a hand and says, 'Well, I would like to say that if your sister wants to be a good citizen and help an Absolver out, I think it is her decision.'

'You stay out of it,' Mikhail mutters. 'We don't even know you.'

'Well, I'm something of an expert—'

'Expert my ass,' Mikhail interrupts him and turns to Danica. 'Listen, I know what this is about. You feel guilty about leaving Father in the mine.'

'It isn't about that,' Danica answers defensively.

'It *is*,' Mikhail exclaims. ' I've been godawful about it too. And I'm sorry for ... for telling everyone that it was your fault.' His expression is wrenched with guilt. 'You don't deserve that.'

Almost imperceptibly, Mr Oraculi nods.

'But you can't let your guilt blind you to the fact that this drunkard over here is grossly incompetent and wouldn't even know where to start looking for our father—'

'But you were *right*,' Danica says. 'I did abandon him there.'

'No, I wasn't—'

'You have seen Mother,' Danica whispers tightly.

Mikhail is silent.

'We need him back,' she speaks without thinking. She speaks, and the words come straight from her—that dark, desperate place in her heart. The place where Beris weeps continuously into the little hours of the night, where Sasha periodically refuses to touch her food, where Mikhail comes home bruised and distant and so black with anger and loneliness that it is as if he is not even there. And in that place, in that part of Danica, it sometimes feels as if Mother's sickness had spread beyond her throat. That the veins had crept from beyond her pale skin, slipped down her bed and climbed each room, each wall, each one of them.

Her sickness is their sickness. Her darkness is their darkness.

*And we are all choking*, she thinks.

Mr Oraculi releases a great big exhale. 'Oh dear. Listen, listen you two.' Mr Oraculi wipes something from his eyes. 'Did I mention that I am willing to share the reward? You won't have to do anything terribly hard either. You just come down with me to the Myshkin Mine, use your special little ears to let me know where that thing that wants to lop our heads off is hiding and I'll take care of the rest. I mean, even if your father is off to the better place, I'm sure you could use the coin, if nothing else.'

Mikhail glares at Mr Oraculi, and then, when looking at Danica he says, 'I suppose he could have made it to the underground deposits. And if he has,' Mikhail says carefully, 'he might have had enough ...'

Enough what? Mikhail's eyes seem to sceptically finish the sentence for him. Water? Food? Air?

Mr Oraculi persists. 'I'll pay well.'

'You'll pay *half*,' Mikhail says and Danica is flushed with relief. '*If we accept.*'

'Half?' Mr Oraculi echoes.

The fact that he is not downright laughing stuns Danica. Is he considering it? Is he seriously considering sharing half of this immeasurable amount with two adolescents? Danica had never even seen more than fifty pence silver in the same place. One thousand sounds like an imaginary number. Mikhail and her look at each other with a similar degree of awe and shock etched on their faces.

Mr Oraculi the Absolver stands up, and for a moment Danica is certain he is about to leave.

He extends his palm to her instead and nods severely. 'You have yourself a deal.'

Mr Oraculi stands beneath the wooden scaffold sealing the mine. His pale skin is slick with sweat, and his thin travel coat sticks to his arms and waist. The fierce sunlight bears down on him. The sycamores rise high behind the Myshkin Mine, blotting the blue skies like blood clots.

He does not make an impressive sight. There is something about Mr Oraculi that keeps Danica on edge. He has the buzzing restlessness of a wasp, floating in and out of a room.

'Excellent, you're here. I've alerted the mayor to our little excursion and—'

'Hold on,' Danica says. 'We have some questions.'

'Yes,' Mikhail says. 'We want to know your plan.'

'The plan?' Mr Oraculi shrugs. 'I've told you. You go into the mine with me, and your special little sister lets me know when the devil, demon, Hassar—whatever you want to call it—is anywhere nearby. And then, obviously, we steer clear.'

'Steer clear?' Mikhail asks. 'Aren't you going to kill it?'

'Goodness gracious,' Mr Oraculi says. 'Kill it? Of course not. Have I mentioned that I'm relatively new in the field? An *apprentice* really, so uh, yeah. No killing, if I can help it.'

Danica and Mikhail share a worried look. 'So why are we going down there?' Danica asks. 'How are you going to deal with the *Hassar* if you aren't going to slay it?'

'I am going to restore the Glyphlight,' the Absolver says matter-of-factly. 'Once we do that, the whole environment will become rather inhospitable for our demonic little friend.' He makes a vague gesture with his hand and a sound that might be intended as an explosion.

The Glyphlight. Danica knows this is how it all started. The Glyphlight went out, and whatever was trapped—or waiting—inside the mine was unleashed.

'And how are you going to do that?' Mikhail asks.

'You see.' Mr Oraculi gestures at the two to follow him. 'Somewhere in this mine there's a big ol' Glyphwall, absolutely spattered with glyphs that would have been sourcing the light. Now I reckon that the glyphs, being fussy little shites, are simply out.'

'Out of what?' Mikhail asks.

'That's complicated.'

'And what if it isn't there?'

'We leave,' Mr Oraculi says happily. 'Fast.'

'And if it comes looking for us?' Mikhail says. 'The Hassar?'

Mr Oraculi crouches in front of Danica. Up close, he looks even gaunter. There are purple stains beneath his dark eyes, and with the rosy hue of intoxication gone, the complexion of his skin is not far from that of a corpse. 'Your sister will be in charge of that.'

Mikhail grabs her hand just before they go in.

'If you feel anything,' Mikhail whispers to her, 'you tell me, and we leave.'

She tries to smile, but finds the corners of her mouth pinned to the spot, as her mind begins to fill with an image. It flashes fast through her head—her father's decomposed mouth unhinged into a soulless scream. Then it's gone. When she looks up, Mikhail is looking back at her curiously

'Are you okay Dani?'

She nods. They enter the mine.

---

The darkness of the mine greets Danica again. There is little to see once they leave the lifts. The coarse earth beneath her feet is as black as the distant path ahead. She hears Oraculi stop, and then a sharp whistle followed by a thin *tssss.*

There is light, in front of the Absolver.

The light is bizarre. A strange, amorphous glow that seems neither shaped nor stagnant. A dawn without a sun. The glow wraps around Mr Oraculi, and extends very little past him. Mr Oraculi keeps a ruthless pace. Danica can see him—for he is aglow—but little else. He is a lone shine in a starless night. And so, as he marches ahead, practically running, she and Mikhail rush after him, stomping blindly on the bristly ground.

Mikhail hisses at Mr Oraculi to slow down. He doesn't.

The three of them descend further into the Myshkin Mine. She cannot tell where they are going. She has never gone this deep, but their march feels longer than it should. She is dizzy, following the thin light that Mr Oraculi emits, unable to see anything besides it. She feels drunk on her feet, unable to do anything but desperately stay within range of the diminishing light. Mr Oraculi seems further and further.

Danica struggles more than Mikhail. She trips, her hands touch something coarse, but she cannot decide if it is the rocky wall or the hard ground. Mikhail must hear her most recent tumble, for even before she rises, she can hear him scream,

'Oy! Bastard!'

Danica is on her feet again. She feels his hand grip hers. Her palms are slick with blood, full of open cuts.

'Dani,' Mikhail says softly. 'Are you alright?'

'Mhm.'

'What in the crypts of hell is wrong with this guy? I thought he wanted you to be a lookout, but then he just runs ahead. I can't see a goddamn thing. Where is he even taking us?' He pulls her along and keeps talking. 'Dani, are you feeling it? Are you feeling the *creature* right now? Is it near?'

She shakes her head.

They walk for a long time. Rushing, panting, falling after each miscalculated step. The sides of her stomach burn. The pain is like a knife, constantly probing the space between her ribs. Mikhail is always beside her, she can hear his heart pounding in his breast and his breath whip with panic whenever she stumbles.

She holds onto his presence. To the sound of his exasperation, to his hitches of concern.

Suddenly Mr Oraculi's distant light becomes stagnant. It grows, expanding until it is a thin white blade, cutting the darkness ahead.

Is the light getting bigger?

'He stopped,' Mikhail says. 'Come on!'

They are in a narrow space. The brightness of Mr Oraculi's light is almost uncomfortable. Squinting, Danica surveys the tunnel. She sees coarse ground and dark rock walls, with jagged stones jutting from the side like hidden blades. There's a dark stain on the jagged stone. Blood.

She realises they were already *here*, but rather than speak she feels as if a hole had been ripped open inside her gut. She tries again, but her voice is trapped beneath the weight of a realisation far darker than the one she is incapable of uttering out loud.

Mikhail grabs Mr Oraculi. 'What in the seven basements of hell is wrong with you? Why did you bring us here if you're just going to run away like that? Are you nuts? Is this all a joke to you?'

Mr Oraculi is indifferent to the boy holding his arm. The glow hisses from his skin like vapour. When he speaks, bright steam spills out of his mouth. 'You can feel it. Can't you?'

She can.

'Hey! Leave her out of it, I'm talking to you—'

Mr Oraculi wrenches his arm free from Mikhail and with a second, swift swing of his arm tosses the boy onto the ground. Mikhail bolts back up almost instantly, but rather than go at the man again he drifts towards Danica, face knotted in anger.

'We were here already,' Danica whispers.

'What?'

'The blood on the rock.' Danica holds up her lacerated hands. 'That's me.'

Mikhail stares at her in pale disbelief. But Danica turns to Mr Oraculi instead. She feels a tremor shift from her spine to her jutting left leg. Carefully, she says, 'You've been walking us in circles, Mr Oraculi.'

He nods.

She doesn't need to ask why. She knows. She had felt it for a while now. Lingering beneath. The stalker, in the dark. They had been used as bait. She, and Mikhail. The Absolver had been dragging them around in circles, as if they were a pair of unknowing worms at the end of a hook. And now, now he stopped.

Danica's stomach felt as if a piece of it had been gnawed out. Her face twists despite her desperation to keep a calm expression.

'You're incredible,' Mr Oraculi whispers, and his glowing, steaming face takes on a strange awe. 'I can barely sense it, even now. And you—from so far away—'

'You could feel it?' Mikhail interrupts. 'So what was this? About helping us find our father? About sharing the reward with us? Were we just ... what ... a—'

'A distraction,' Mr Oraculi answers. 'A necessary one.'

'You're frightened,' Danica says suddenly. 'Even though you're an Absolver, you're frightened of the creature that lives here. That's why you wanted us to come. You wanted a distraction while you deal with the Glyphlight. You're afraid.'

'Terrified,' Mr Oraculi admits with a smile. 'And for what it's worth to you,' he says as he slowly retreats. ' I am truly, truly sorry.'

'You bastard!' Mikhail howls. 'You fucking—'

Mr Oraculi clicks his fingers, and the light disappears. A windfall of darkness washes over the cavern. They hear his footsteps recede but neither of them moves after him. In the overwhelming blackness that remains, the two siblings remain frozen. Danica cannot see, the terror that grips her is immutable. It crushes all and any other thought.

She is helpless, alone and in her heart of hearts she knows that Mr Oraculi has left them *now* because something else is drawing near.

'He left us here,' Mikhail says. 'The bastard actually left us here!'

'I'm sorry *Misha*,' Danica murmurs pathetically, 'it is all my fault, I wanted to come down here—'

'Can you hear it, Danica?' Her brother squeezes her palm. 'The creature?' he asks, once she is calmer. 'Is it nearing us?'

'I think so.'

'Which way?'

'It's hard to explain.'

'Can you take us *away* from it?'

'I can try.'

The warnings pound in her ears. She thinks, dreads, that she can hear stone-crunching slithers from above. The tension in her head pulls through the muscles of her back, crawls around her stomach and explodes. In her stupefied silence, she realises that Mikhail is waiting for her to lead the way.

*Slither-slither.*

The sound has got the pattern of a leak. Drip—drip—drip—drip. She cannot accurately locate it, but she can tell which way it is *not.*

She goes and Mikhail holds her hand. Neither can see a thing. Her steps feel strangely light. She cannot tell when ground will meet her foot, and when it does, it comes to her as a surprise. She hears the shuffle of their feet, the earth they drag, and listens desperately for the dweller in the dark.

Mikhail is silent. Perhaps he does not wish to interrupt her concentration. Perhaps his terror is as numbingly ghoulish as her own.

After a few minutes, Danica stops. Again, an image sears through her brain—her father's face, decomposed, maggot-filled and rotting—it is the same image she had seen before entering the mine. Earlier it was a flash. Quick. Merciful.

Now it lingers.

Danica does not scream. She remains still. She is in utter darkness now, holding hands with her brother. He asks her why she has stopped.

Her father is before her; his hands are a bloodless grey and crisscrossed with pulpy black veins. He is reaching out for her, mouth agape in that same heart-rending scream—Danica trembles. She is unable to speak, nor is she able to warn her brother of the horror inside her mind. She feels small, and meaningless, in ways that make the cords inside her throat shrivel into lifeless, rotten things.

'Dani? What's going on? Are you feeling the creature? Answer me, Danica. Why aren't you moving forward? What are you feeling? Danica, please, don't just stand there. Look at me, look at me right now. I know you can't see me, but I am here. Dani—Dani ... Dani!'

Danica sees, again and again, visions of her father. In all of them he is a decomposed, wretched creature. A half-living abomination stitched together from the pieces that had once made him whole.

*Slither-slither.*

She sees his eyes. Golden flashfires shooting through the dark. The brightness of his eyes illuminates the vague shape beneath them. Long, crooked limbs. The darkness around those eyes is different. The creature beneath it is different. A hunched-forward silhouette.

'Danica!'

Her brother is crushing her fingers. When she turns to him, he is not looking at her.

He can see the creature too.

'Dani!' Mikhail nearly yanks her arm out of her socket. 'Run!'

Danica runs without seeing the path ahead. She stumbles and falls. Her brother picks her up. They flee, surrounded by a blinding darkness. As she runs her mind is weighted down with terrible thoughts. How did she think this creature to be her father? This ghoulish, monstrous abomination? This nightmare incarnate? She cannot see Mikhail, it is only the force of his grip that keeps her going. They scrape against the walls of the mine, stumble on the scattered rocks and cut their flesh on the sharp edges.

'Keep going Dani! Keep Going!—' Mikhail lurches forward and loses his grip on her hand. She hears a loud *thump* followed by a long, heart-wrenching skid and the sound of a person rolling down a long slope.

'Mikhail!'

She hears a truly miserable groan, distant as if coming from the bottom of a well.

Without thinking, Danica lowers herself to the ground and extends her legs forward, sitting on the ground. There is indeed a slope ahead, and it is steep. She slides herself slowly down it, using her palms to de-escalate her descent.

*Slither-slither-slither.*

The sharp, scattered rocks along the slope bite into her flesh. She slides further down the slope, blind and hurt and choked with the fear of the creature following her. She claws into the dark.

She hears something. Soft, pained whimpers. Once, when she was younger, their dog Tesso had been lured from the safety of their home to the nearby woods. Father had told Danica that it was the scent of the she-wolf that had lured Tesso out of his senses. When Danica and Mother found him, he was moaning in a puddle of blood under a fallen sycamore, every piece of him gnawed or chomped or ripped open.

When Danica finds her brother's bloody leg, and hears his pitiful whines of pain, she remembers Tesso that day, after the wolves got him.

'*Misha*?' Her voice cracks in her mouth. 'Are you okay?'

His leg shifts out of her hold. He is rolling on the ground, suppressing his own screams. The muted sound of his pained moans breaks her heart.

'We'll get you out of here, Misha.' She tries to find him. 'Please, please, let's go.'

He groans again, and then his voice changes, breaks into a childish, helpless sob. She tries to calm him, to ascertain the degree of his injury, but she doesn't know what to do, she does not know where to touch or how to ease his pain.

His crying is unbearable now. He weeps inconsolably. Her older brother. And she can do nothing for him.

'We'll get out of here, Misha.' she wipes her own tears. 'I promise I'll get you out of here.'

'D-D-D ... D-Da ...'

Her voice frightens her. She tries to pick him up. 'Come on, Misha ... come on ...'

'Dad ... Dad ...'

'Where?'

She turns around once more. There is nothing there.

No.

She sees it now. In the darkness. Two gold-yellow glints. Eyes? It seems impossible. She cannot stop looking, cannot stop staring into the golden abyss. She feels its presence, its proximity. She had not heard it come.

And then, light.

It explodes through the mine, pulsing from the distant tunnels and through the gigantic cavern. The light shoots forward, wraps around Danica and Mikhail and suffuses the bottom of the slope with shimmering radiance.

The Glyphlight! It's back! Mr Oraculi was not lying. He reactivated the glyphs in the mine.

She sees the creature. Truly *sees* it.

The Glyphlight barely reaches her. It is a great big sphere of radiance, but it has a clear, undeniable limit. A border between light and dark. Beyond that border, she sees the Hassar.

Its limbs are excessively long, triple jointed and corrupted with the most heinous rot. The torn remains of a miner's blouse cling to bone-thin shoulders and strips of leather remain wrapped around green-black decomposed feet.

It is her father who is looking down at her. He is taller than he had ever been, as if someone had stretched him across a tanning rack. There are boils all over his face, white, bulbous ulcers on his stomach and pockets of abscesses along his neck. He is undeniably her father, but he is also a nightmare creature, leering at her through sickly yellow eyes, mouth wide in a soulless gape.

Danica stares back at him, paralysed.

Danica's father speaks,

'*Leave him ... here.*'

Danica is too stunned to think. It was a figment of her imagination. It must have been. She reaches for her brother and tries to wrap his arms around her—

'*LEAVE ... HIM ... HERE ...*'

The creature that was once her father is leering at her now. He is hunched over so low that the tip of his decomposed chin is level with her face. She can feel the sting of its stench against her eyes. The glow of the Glyphlight stands between them. The Hassar does not enter the light. There is a dark, twisted joy in his golden eyes. His rotten, gaping mouth twists into a depraved grin.

The Glyphlight line begins to retreat.

'Misha!' Danica cries out. 'What's happening?'

She looks around her. The Glyphlight is withdrawing away from the creature. Is it the creature's doing? Is it Mr Oraculi?

'I d-don't know ...' Mikhail stammers.

'Why?'

Mikhail does not answer. His bloodless face is wrought with exhaustion. In the light, she can see the extent of his bleeding. His leg is twisted into an unnatural shape, and beneath the mangled red flesh there is the barest glint of white bone. Danica is sick to her stomach. She understands, in a numb sort of way, that something is wrong with the glyph or that perhaps that they are too far from it.

As the line between shadow and light retracts, their father advances towards them.

Danica tries to lift her brother. He screams. The pain in his face makes her heart stop. She suppresses the awful feeling and slides her arms beneath him.

He is heavy and she cannot even lift him off the ground.

'*LEAVE ... HIM ... HERE ...*'

Mikhail is not looking at her anymore. His terrified eyes are glued to the walking corpse of their father. Danica tries to snap him out of it, to get him to talk, to get him to tell her what to do. When her brother finally comes to his senses, he looks at her with a tortured grimace and says, 'Danica ... he ... he will get you ... please ... go ...'

No.

'I'm not leaving you here!' she replies. 'Come on, let's go!'

'Dani please—'

She covers her ears.

She had already left her father. Her brother had wanted to look for him. And if they had? Would they have found *him* or this creature? Perhaps if they found him when the blood was fresh, like Bojan, their father could have been spared this fate. This terrible, grotesque transformation. And if she left Mikhail? What would become of him? Would Mikhail also become possessed by this creature? Would he spend the rest of his days as this decomposed monstrosity?

A monstrous vision of Mikhail and Father walking side by side as two ghouls burns through Danica, and she cries out.

The light continues to ebb away. Father remains just outside of it. Patient. Eager. He is as close as he can be without actually stepping into it. The edges of the light slice the air in front of his grotesque face.

So close.

Almost inside the light.

Danica steps away from her brother. His eyes are full of tears and so are hers. There is a dejectedness to him now. 'Go,' Mikhail says. 'Go Dani ...'

She turns to her father. He is watching, waiting. Soon he will be able to reach Mikhail and drag him into the darkness. Danica knows that she isn't able to carry her brother up the slope. She knows the Glyphlight would be gone before they can escape.

She understands now what she has to do.

'Father,' she says softly.

The creature that was once her father grins maniacally at the sound of her voice. A thick black substance bubbles on his putrid lips and dribbles down his chin. He is eager for her to leave her brother behind, but he also watches her with deranged thrill in his shining yellow eyes. As if the sight of her, the sound of her voice—the nearness of her—are all too succulent a treat to pass up. And so, as she comes closer, the deformed monstrosity moves with her.

She approaches the creature. Her advance is slow, staggering from left to right as she plods towards the darkness.

It watches her hungrily as she eliminates the gap between them. Yellow, glowing eyes, shifting left and right like a pendulum to match Danica's movements. She stands so close to it now that they nearly touch.

One shrouded in darkness, the other bathed in Glyphlight.

'Danica!' Mikhail screams. 'What are you doing?'

'I shouldn't have left you here,' Danica says to the creature, ignoring her brother. 'I should have come looking for you, like Mikhail wanted.'

Closer.

'I am sorry, father,' she says, and the deformed demon is salivating at the sight of her, not hearing her words, not moving with her anymore. It watches her with a predatory single-mindedness. Ready to wrap her in shadows and bury her in the bottom of the void.

Closer.

She knows how vulnerable she is. The creature does, too. She steps forward, her feet cross the line between light and darkness.

'I'm sorry,' she tells what remains of her father.

The creature's obscene face twists with reckless delight. It lunges forward before she can finish her step.

Its desperation is its undoing.

Danica retracts her foot and leaps backwards. The creature realises, but it is too late. Its long black limbs wrap around her, crooked fingers dig into her flesh and the face—distorted, grotesque and at this point in no way like her father's—is right in front of her, ready to sink its teeth.

But she is within the Glyphlight now. They are *both* within the Glyphlight.

The creature that had pretended to be her father spasms and writhes and screeches in what can only be immeasurable agony. Its long limbs swing as if it is trying to swim, wild and mad and tortured. The light swallows the creature, and wherever it touches the flesh sears and hisses and burns.

The creature turns on its side to crawl out of the light.

Danica does not let it. She wraps herself around its gigantic arm and holds onto it. It whips her around, screeching and howling, and for a moment she thinks that the creature will toss her into the earth and escape the Glyphlight—but the creature does not.

Mikhail is opposite her, holding the monstrosity by its legs.

Its final, dying howls pierce through Danica like a knife, and the pain explodes in the back of her head. Mikhail is sobbing, his mouth drawn into a wretched, miserable grimace.

Neither sibling releases their grip.

---

When the surgeon takes out his cutting tools, Mother gasps and hurries Sasha and Beris to the room upstairs. Danica stays with Mikhail.

The deed is quick, and Mikhail is unconscious for most of it. The surgeon doesn't ask for payment but when Danica escorts him to the door he tells her that what she has done was an amazing thing, carrying her injured brother out of the mine. He then pauses looking at the door.

'I knew your father by the way,' he starts. 'Not well, mind you, but enough to know that he was a good person. I'm sorry he's gone.'

'Me too.'

When she goes to the village to ask if anyone had seen Mr Oraculi, no one even knows who he is. Even the barmaids at the *Ragged Stoat* seem strangely forgetful of the man.

Her brother's stump heals nicely in the following days. Mother makes him a bright red sash which he wraps around the stub. In fact, she also knits a woollen hat for Sasha and a pair of little green mittens for Beris. She is unexpectedly active. Her health seems to improve, although the garish black veins on her pale throat show no signs of receding.

At least they do not advance.

Danica thinks that it is Mother's sheer willpower that keeps them at bay. Her mother knows, Danica thinks, that Mikhail needs her. Moreso than ever before. On some nights, however, when Danica looks long and hard at those dark veins, she thinks that there is something different about them. Less menacing than they were before Mikhail and Danica had returned to the mine.

It is on one such night that Mikhail, while Danica replaces the dressing of his stump, first broaches the idea of telling the truth to their mother.

'You mean about Father?' Danica asks.

'Yes.'

'Maybe.' Danica tightens the dressing. 'Does it hurt?'

'A little.'

She loosens it.

'I mean,' Mikhail continues. 'Don't you think she deserves to know what happened to him?' His voice chokes. 'What he *became*?'

'That wasn't him.'

'How can you be so sure?'

Danica shrugs. The truth is that she doesn't know. The creature in the cave could have been her father for all she knew. It looked like him, in a twisted, monstrous sort of way. And yet Danica feels little doubt in her heart when she turns to her brother and affectionately squeezes his hand. 'I just know.'

Mikhail smiles.

The siblings stiffen as they both hear footfalls outside the door. A moment later they hear their mother's scream.

Mikhail nearly flips over his chair but Danica rushes to the door. Her mother is on her knees, tears flowing down her cheeks. When she sees Danica, her breath hitches and a great bright smile spreads on her sobbing face. 'Oh, oh *Dani …*'

There's a wooden strongbox on the ground just outside their door. Later, when they've counted it for the umpteenth time, Mother victoriously confirms that there are indeed two thousand silverpence inside—twice what had been initially promised to them.

There is also a note. It is addressed to her.

Danica reads twice.

*Tell me: would you like to become an Absolver?*

*– Mr Oraculi*

# The Traitor

by Paddy Boylan

Across the seas of dunes. Past jagged mountains shaped and sharpened by the winds of years, and by true oceans long since vanished into myth. Past the collapsing faces of ruins that rear, half-emerged, from receding tidal sands—only to be buried once again as the epoch slowly breathes. A lone sandship ploughs through desert night.

The clan within is thirty families strong. A trading clan, and one of many sired by the tribe Dust Flag. Tonight, this clan is fleeing.

It has been days since they pulled at full speed away from port. They'd half-expected to see warships by now—the telltale blue sails and the dust clouds of their treads, shimmering up out of the heat haze behind them. But as they roll on into their third night, there is still no sign of pursuit. Finally, they are beginning to breathe easy. They feel lucky to have escaped the worst.

But this is a mistake. Wary as they've been for signs of grand threat, they've left no contingency for subtler dangers, and a small company of riders—only seven; all that is required—is drawing nearer every hour, saddled upon desert reptiles that will give no sign of approach.

They'll realise soon enough.

The exchange was going so well; soon Port Echo's markets would be overflowing with the cargo they unloaded. Boxes and palettes and sacks and canisters of fresh water, dark coffee beans, exotic fruits and precious oils, of the leathers and pearls and spun, glistening threads of enormous desert molluscs hunted or herded (a variety of which—great shelled macropods, docile and contented—are still stabled in their hold).

And for all this: silver. Sapphires. The arcana of another age, wondrous artefacts found when the tides of sand are at their lowest. And the assurances, bound in writing, of future trade to come.

But when the winds of war come howling, those straddling the border between powers are so often swept away. How many tales are told of folk caught by circumstance in that widening gulf—traders, adventurers, emissaries, star-crossed lovers? So, so many; few with happy endings.

It's the very reason the oral traditions are sacrosanct: to remember such lessons.

And so our merchant clan had a difficult choice to make.

It will be hard now, knowing just how much they'd forfeited, left piled high upon the dock, and all the traded wealth that could have been. Their margins are already modest; it could take years of rationing, and careful planning, and trading what they can for what they must, to see this kind of bounteous surplus again. If they ever see it again.

But not a single life was lost in the escape. And their clanship, the *Northstar* (a beautiful old sanctuary engine, even now enshrining itself in desert folklore), is intact, save a peppering of fresh scars around its tracks—a parting gift of bullets, though only a scratch to the old pilgrim, and an easy repair.

Times ahead will be hard, but all the easier knowing that their families, and those they keep like family, are safe and close at hand.

At least there is that.

Their elders tell them this: *be grateful for all you have.*

Both moons are out tonight. Shya, and her younger sister Taerin, bathe the sands with their pale splendour, the ship below so small against the vast and star-glittered sky. A clear night like this, with the whole nimbus of creation spread wide above and blessed by both the sister moons, ought to be a time of good omen. But the clan inside wishes only for blackness.

The *Northstar* is running dark. All of its myriad lights are out, though the lunar glow might still betray them. Its silhouette is like that of a great citadel against the dark sky, albeit one that's left its city, stealing away on caterpillar track in the night. Its dust cloud only compounds the problem—the long tail of a slow and landbound comet. The passing of its treads bears sand as moonlit powder high into the air, dispersing it to settle gently behind them, or to carry on the high winds to distant lands beyond.

Then there's the noise. On a calm night like this (and with the brisk pace they're keeping), a sandship's engines can be heard a half-horizon's span away. Close enough, you feel it beneath your feet. Closer still, in your bones.

It is by these means that their hunters have found them.

Perched atop a stony mesa, the seven riders listen, and watch, out over the darkened dunes as the shape of their prey draws slowly larger. They rest at ease in their saddles, collecting themselves in the last minutes of calm before the work begins. The reptiles that kneel languidly beneath them are lithe and bipedal things, their forms like flightless, featherless birds—swift and predatory.

At last the sandship passes by, and the riders peel off, one by one, riding down a narrow path to fall in with the dust cloud of its wake.

For all the stealth that running dark affords a vessel, that cloak of shadow carries a dangerous flaw: it blinds you beyond your peripheries. Radiance gone, skulkers can advance to within dangerously close distances. Can attach themselves like ticks.

Just so.

The seven riders are patient, following closely behind the ship—but now the terrain is changing, soft dunes giving way to stones and stout, urthen pillars (and the occasional islands of rock, detached to drift as urthbergs under some unknown, motive force). The ship slows, relying all the more on nocturnal sensors to grope slowly ahead.

Yes—this is the place.

One of the riders, gifted with night eyes like a desert fox, pulls ahead of the others until they ride at the dust cloud's barest fading edge: just enough to spy two tiny figures—sentries—high upon the upper deck, silhouetted by the moonlight. The pair lean idly against the railing; talking, staring out into the night sky, oblivious to the rider that is watching them far below. A minute passes before they turn, and wander the deck's perimeter to its far opposite side.

The rider signals back to the others—a raised arm, four fingers extended.

Now all seven spur their steeds, the reptiles' flaring nostrils gouting plumes of dust and grit as they gather pace. Quickly now, emerging from the vessel's wake to close in with its portside, a few cautious yards kept between themselves and those massive, grinding tracks. As they fall in with their quarry's speed, six draw brass crossbows and gossamer cables. The seventh will remain behind and keep the company's steeds from straying.

The six rise in their saddles, balancing on the stirrups, pointing their crossbows high. The dark is no obstacle—they know exactly where to aim.

Amongst them is a narrow-shouldered man. His face is gaunt, his eyes recessed. The others turn to face him. He gestures his command: two fingers pointing.

*Go.*

Six bolts sail high, hinged flukes releasing to catch the upper deck's railing, eight floors above. Each firer tests their line—short, sharp tugs. The lines are good.

The narrow-shouldered man smiles beneath his sandscarf, the slightest curl at the edges of thin lips. The smile he wears when things go *just so.*

He signals to the others. The boarding commences.

Sharah is first over the top—a young and eager killer. Lizardhide boots pad softly onto the deck, desert cloak fluttering around her like the wings of a great and settling moth. She crouches low, taking her spear from her back and kissing its haft: the familiar ritual of a favoured weapon. The other five ascend silently behind her. They glide like ghosts along the upper deck, closing upon the two sentries. The pair are brother and sister—barely adults.

No one hears the six approaching. No one hears the sentries' muffled screams as hands grip their faces, and steel punctures their bodies. No one hears the two lifeless forms, tipped over the side, falling to the sands below. Lost to the shifting dunes, no one will ever find them.

Sharah moves to take point. Her weapon is still dry. She'd watched her comrades as they cut the pair down, all the dark fluid spilling from the wounds, and it galls her. She has made a pact with herself: tonight, she will be distinguished. So now she paces ahead of them, hoping for another living opportunity.

But soon she halts, and turns to gesture: three fingers drawn across. She's found a doorway, left wide open. And she shakes her head. She already has utter contempt for these soft-bodied parasites, hiding in the walls like grubs. But this carelessness? She can scarcely believe it.

Though the man with the narrow shoulders can. He knows these folk aren't warriors. They're barely disciplined. And they've been running for days now, no doubt exhausted by a constant, heightened vigil, waiting anxiously for pursuers from his tribe, Thousand Spears, to appear from over the horizon and deliver unto them the wrath they'd hoped to evade.

No wrath had come. And so gradually, inevitably, they'd started to relax.

The narrow-shouldered man's name is Tel'zat, and tonight is like so many in his furtive, blood-soaked life. Except that on this night, he is leader.

He knows that people are spring coils: a little danger and they wind up tight, practically trembling with potential action. But leave them undisturbed, and slowly, slowly, those coils relax, all that trembling energy bleeding away. And then, finally, when again they're calm, believing all the worst is behind them ...

Tel'zat signals. The six enter the ship.

---

Tel'zat is first inside, followed by Juro, a man wearing a metal mask. He is Tel'zat's second, though many years his senior. The room they step into is lightless, and the pair draw twine-bound luminspheres, pale orbs to peel the dark like the sister moons in miniature. Light passes over shelves lined with canned rations, copper wire, dusty ornaments, bundles of fabric. One corner has a shrine, draped in wilted flowers, honouring unknown ancestors.

As the others fan out, Tel'zat takes a corner of the fabric in one gloved hand, turning it over. A pattern graces its edge: a beautiful filigree of bramble and thorn, in a pleasing embroidered tangle. Casting his light slowly now, that same pattern is etched into the polished timber of the walls.

Leaning close, he can distinguish little scenes of desert life amongst the twisting bramble: etched clouds and suns; great molluscs—tube wurms, grown to colossal size—diving in the sands; snaking processions of cloaked pilgrims in profile, treading a long and sacred journey to some far and secret place. And indulging further, he removes his glove to trace the outlines with the bare tips of his fingers.

Once, Thousand Spears had basked in the worked elegance of a hundred conquered tribes. The rightful tribute of the weak unto the strong, as ever it should be. In those days they'd revelled in beauties myriad in kind and materials, proof in their abundance of the breadth and variety of the peoples conquered. But all that changed. Now the expected posture is scorn for these works. For their frivolity, and their weakness.

There's something else. Something about these etchings. Something balanced right on the edge of recollection ...

Juro is staring at him.

'If you would honour us with your attention, *Jan'tai.*'

Tel'zat still isn't used to the title. Jan'tai—warrior nobility. An appointment Juro no doubt thought should have gone to one more like himself. He hadn't hidden his resentment then, and he doesn't hide it now. With that metal face he looks like a spectre, conjured in judgement out of the darkness.

Juro's mask is a perfect curve of tsaltalloy, smooth and featureless, save a straight line of visionslit. Usually reflective, like a polished golden mirror, tonight it is dulled with ashes. Such masks are the honour (and obligation) of Thousand Spears warriors headed into open battle, but old Juro wears his always. A sarcophagus for his face.

He already has the map of the ship—a tattered, yellowed vellum—unfurled in his hands, as he patiently waits for his esteemed jan'tai to stop ... whatever it is he thinks he's doing. Messing with distractions. The others are spooling cable or checking equipment or anything else to seem like they don't notice.

Tel'zat doesn't care. But all the same, he redons his glove.

'Gather,' he says, gaining the attention they're pretending isn't already on him. Their eyes drawn, he points to a spot on Juro's map. He tracks a finger across the tangle of crisscrossed details, finally stopping at a small square. 'Us.' He then follows the lines of an adjoining corridor as it snakes around, around, and up to the ship's highest point. 'The bridge.' And then down, down to the lower decks. 'Engine room.'

He points to two of his warriors: Sharah (listening at the interior door, still clutching her spear), and—Kyar? Kwar? He'd never bothered to learn the name. 'With me,' he says, 'to the bridge.'

Sharah's posture grows taller. 'I will not disappoint you,' she says. Tel'zat does not acknowledge her.

He points to old Juro, and the remaining two: 'To the engine room.'

Then he draws a silver watch from his desert cloak, and Juro does the same. Each is bespoke, and detailed, and suspended from a delicate chain. Pretty things, made by Dust Flag artisans, no less. Tel'zat enjoys that irony. Each twists the tiny dials until the hands of the watches match, perfectly synchronised. Then he looks up at the masked veteran.

'Seven minutes—no more. Take it quickly. When I give my order from the bridge, lock down the doors.' The masked face nods its obedience.

Then, to the rest: 'Control the beast's brain, and its beating heart, and we control its course.' *Then the next phase begins*, he thinks. *And six will have conquered a hundred.* And he's wearing his thin smile again.

They already know the plan, of course. They'd studied it unto tedium. But in truth, Tel'zat only trusts himself, even if he admits that they're reliable enough. Juro most of all; the old veteran is an asset (if obviously resentful of his command). Sharah, least. She's too young, and talented as she may be, that impulse to kill—so common to the youth of their tribe—is far too strong. But she's favoured of a warlord; he doesn't know which. So he'll keep her leash short, and suffer her for now.

If Tel'zat could live as the predators of the desert, without need for kin or kind, he'd cast off his pretenses like so many rotten rags. But he can't. So he keeps their covenants.

He looks over his infiltrators, standing ready. They will need to be swift, and precise. There is precious little room for error, and if any part is fumbled, escape will not be guaranteed. But the plan is good—after all, he is its architect. The lion's share of glory will be his.

'Let us begin,' he says.

---

Six pass into the corridor beyond, and then split: three travelling north, three south, quiet as unforeseen calamity. Juro leads one group, Tel'zat the second, Sharah close by his side. The way ahead in both directions alternates from dark to dusk-coloured glow, the dimmed interior of a ship under stealth.

Though, even in the half-light, the inside seems comfortable. Even cosy—all the drabness of 'ship as machine for moving' dressed with the furnishings of a home. The smell of incense and spices, and faintest hashish, hide the must and engine oil. The portals branching to either side are painted the bright hues of verdancy, or sunrise, or with cool, deep blues, and beaded curtains clack gently with the slow undulations of the clan's journey.

A passing scent of cooking. The muted sound of children's laughter. A pale violet cat that wanders into the corridor, arcing to hiss as it spots them, before darting away.

Every thirty paces the three stop, hiding and listening at a bulkhead door, armoured thick in case of fire or intruders. But all are unsealed.

And then up ahead—as they linger at the seventh bulkhead. Voices.

'... only enough drinking gallons for the week. I don't mind going a little thirsty, but for my daughter? We should never have agreed to trade any of it, let alone *half*. All that water, just left for those lizardfondling tickfarms ...'

The hidden infiltrators go still. But Sharah's stillness is dangerous—a perched hawk that's just spotted its prey.

'It's done, Ghani,' says a second voice. 'And your daughter will be fine. We'll all be fine. The markets at Akurad will trade us springwater for a favour and a whisker. We're known there.'

A creak, to Tel'zat's left. It's Sharah's leather-shod grip, clenching tight around the haft of her spear. She glances at him with eyes wide and bright and expectant in the shadows. *Can we kill them?* they ask. *Please let us kill them.*

He gestures his refusal, sharp and definite. His ears tell him they're already passing off into some adjoining chamber. There's no danger here. Can she not tell that? No—she can; it just doesn't interest her.

He knows her kind. So eager to prove martial prowess. Some of them even achieve it: many are jan'tai, though called on for very different tasks to Tel'zat. And some—fewer—live as grand avatars of war. But most die young. And none understand discretion.

They wait out the moments there until the voices have disappeared deeper into the vessel and away from concern. Sharah's eyes track them the whole way.

They move on.

At the bend ahead they spy the stairs to the ninth deck. They're close now. They ascend them carefully, crouching low at the apex to scan the length of the hall beyond. And for the second time that night, Tel'zat's gaze catches on that beguiling, familiar pattern—briars, thorns, little pilgrim figures—this time laced into the borders of a wurmsilk tapestry, nearly as tall as he is. It hangs from the wall, its platinum thread shimmering with the slightest movements of his head.

In anyone else, he'd judge these lapses of attention—allowing himself to be distracted so—as grave ineptitude. He knows this. But he is he, and he'll do as he pleases.

Where does he know the pattern from? He'll dismiss it, for now. Merely an appealing design. *Either way*, he thinks, *when my work here is done, I'm coming back for this.*

The others see him studying it. He pays them no notice.

He draws his watch. Four minutes remain. The anticipation grows.

And there, on the next corner, is the confirmation that their map had been true. Cresting the wide, ascending staircase ahead is the command deck entrance. The *Northstar's* vulnerable brain, prophesied in the diagrams of a tattered vellum that cost only a chip of glassy sapphire. How many times over will that map have paid for itself? How many thousands? The way is open, and it is unguarded.

Gently they creep up those stairs until they hear the muted babble of command from within. Crouching, flanking the doorway on either side, they steal a careful glance—the room beyond is wide and shadowy, lit only by the soft aurora of electronics. They count no more than ten figures, mostly seated and turned towards their instruments, or gazing out to the starry darkness beyond the room's single, expansive window. The giant's primary eye.

Tel'zat closes his own two eyes and breathes the air—the smell of the moment. He wants to savour what is about to come.

---

Beyond the glass the night is quiet and clear. Enchanted beneath the moons, the land itself seems to coolly luminesce, and in the interplay of light and shadow its stony columns adopt dreamy and anthropic forms. Here, a woman bathing; there, a child at play; the ship moving amongst them like a wanderer in a statue garden, as the figures slowly animate with the drift of its perspective.

The crew within the bridge can watch in contemplation. They're far from Port Echo now, and those who sought to harm them. They are transitioning at last from an uncertain present, towards a hopeful future, and inward to those dreamy spaces that live outside of time's concern. They're travelling through such a space right now.

The room's air is warm and familiar, and gently alive as it hums with the devices around them: navigation, signalling, sensors and the inputs and outputs of chatter between decks. The give and take of shipborne life. All is well with the world.

And then a sound—the shunt and clack of a lever. The pneumatic hiss of armoured doors, sealing the chamber like a tomb. As the crew turn and see their trespassers—as they pale and go wild-eyed, and open mouths to scream—it is far too late.

Curved blades lash from under dune-coloured cloaks, slashes casting hot sprays across the floor, and walls, and the chamber's broad windows. Panels that gave soft blues and whites a moment ago now wash the room in crimson. Some raise desperate arms in their defence. Some rise to flee, but there is nowhere in the room to run.

Sharah lets forth a wild laugh. Her spear hasn't left her grip, not once, since they'd boarded the *Northstar* together. It had become almost unbearable—the weight of all that inertia. Now she thrusts, and spins, and punctures, and twists, again and again, her world coming alive with all the wicked glee unlocked inside her. Those screams, those sprays; adrenaline soars within her, giving clarity like a brilliant, burning dawn. She is giddy with exhilaration.

A figure emerges from an alcove, raising a weighty powdergun, detailed and decorated, to bear on Sharah—but the gunner is much too slow. A flick of Sharah's hand from her cloak sends a spinning knife that catches them in the eye; and down they go, screaming. Their weapon tumbles to the deck, discharging wild scattershot as they paw and grope at the embedded knife, shrieking like an arrow-struck crow.

Already five are dead or dying, slumped over controls or crumpled to the floor. Those left are trying to recede as far back as back can go, cowering vainly under consoles or pressing into the walls in the half-mad hope that the physical might give way. They can do little else.

When scholars discuss courage, they'll linger on questions such as: *How is it born?* And, usually, they'll agree it's in the crucible of transformative events. A chemistry of pressure, circumstance and psyche. Though sometimes a being—one like Tel'zat, now drawing his sword across the belly of someone screaming for mercy—is simply made with a diminished capacity for fear, and all the more capacity for great and terrible deeds.

But is that truly courage? In the absence of an obstacle there isn't an overcoming.

Amidst the carnage there is a woman, bald-headed and hard-faced, who, though terrified at the steel-edged hurricane that has swept into the room, fights down her panic. Two options now lay before her. Both are hideous.

Her robes are teal-blue, now spattered with red. A jewelled sword is at her hip. Her left forearm ends midway: an ancient injury, and a forever-lesson in discretion and valour. Where one hand should be is a well-crafted hook, and she wears four rings on the other. Precious seconds have fallen away, gone forever as she wrestles with her panic. She will never forgive herself.

So now she fills her lungs and bellows.

*'STOP.'*

That single word, charged with all the years of captain's authority, cuts through the maelstrom. And the blades that started it give pause. Her eyes lock with Tel'zat's, command recognising command.

She lifts her sword by its scabbard. 'I am Captain Jeziar of the *Northstar*.' She tosses it clattering to the floor. 'Cease your attack. I surrender this bridge.'

Sharah reels back from her latest victim, her weapon tracing an arc of ruby droplets. Just a moment ago she was a god of death; she felt like the sun. Now this rude interruption? She turns back to finish her work, but Tel'zat extends a single outstretched palm. She pauses, and the unslain figure at her feet clambers back, whimpering, trailing bloody handprints.

A haunting of moans from the stricken and the dying. The air smells of iron. Tel'zat crouches to wipe his blade on someone's clothes, then stoops to claim the captain's sword. Holding it up, he half draws it from its scabbard, inspecting the blade against a console's pale light. The captain watches his movements, her single fist clenched behind her back, her jaw firm to stop it trembling.

'Jeziar,' he says, turning the sword over, the words said more to it than her.

'Protector of this clan,' she says, 'and master of its ship. Honoured daughter of Dust Flag.' A drop of someone else's blood drips from her brow.

'Protector,' he says, with his cruel little smile that is almost a smirk. Seemingly satisfied with the sword, he sheaths it, finally looking at her. 'I accept your surrender, Captain.' And he stows her blade next to his own. For a very long moment he stares at her, measuring her, searching the captain's eyes for what might lie behind them.

Then he reaches into his cloak, drawing first his luminsphere, and then a folded square of parchment, which he holds out to her, his gaze unblinking.

She hesitates a moment at the monster's offering. But at last she takes the parchment, unfolds it, unfolds it again, revealing under the sphere's light the lines of a faded topography. At first, it's hard to make sense of. An amateur's work. But as her eyes wander its contours she begins to recognise their current area and the upheaval of broken mountains that rise to the near north-west.

Tel'zat points to a tiny triangle of ink: a ravine that cuts a winding scar through the rise. He looks at her. 'This is your destination now.'

At first, she's puzzled by the demand. She knows the spot, of course—the canyon called Meleshab, thought cursed by some travellers. Deep and steep-walled, arches and half-arches of stone curling over it from above like the bone-claws of a giant, eternally poised to peer over into its depths and dredge the living contents with a single scoop of its hand.

And then the awful realisation finds her. It creeps over her body. She knows what awaits them there; the scores of warriors—killers just like these—concealed and patient atop those white stone arches, to descend upon the *Northstar* as it passes below. Swarming down over it, and into it, like ants.

No one outside of this room knows of the carnage that's taken place behind the armoured doors. When would the rest of her clan realise their vessel's course had changed? Would they even question it? Not a single soul beyond this bridge has any idea of the catastrophe that awaits them.

She looks up at him, without expression. 'A trap.'

He only smiles his wicked smile. 'Worse if you don't obey.'

She lets the map flutter to her feet, turning towards the broad deck window behind her, and staring out into the endless sky beyond. Her fist is clenched so tight behind her back it feels as if it might well with blood. Outside she is calm. Inside her mind is fevered and racing, searching for anything—*anything*—that might help them evade what's coming. She gazes into that infinite black for a time that seems far longer than that which passes down here in the world below, until her eyes come to focus on the ghost of her reflection in the glass, staring back.

'You've already taken our cargo,' she says to that glass. 'All of it. What we left at port was all we had—your master knows that. And by the Strife Accords, which I *know* that your tribe—"*honour bound*"—adheres to, you cannot take the *Northstar*. Not a ship that never belonged to you, for some skirmish that we never instigated.' *Unless ...*

She watches over her reflection's shoulder as the killer takes a single step forward.

'But captain,' he says, 'this is no skirmish. Can't you feel it? This is the red hand of war around you now.' He gestures at his two minions, waiting like attack dogs to his either side. 'We are its first finger. It doesn't matter that your clan didn't *instigate* it. It is your tribe, and my tribe, and I don't know or care for the details. But you will be the first to pay its price.'

Her response comes slow. 'And if I refuse?'

'Then we kill your kin. One by one, until they make the choice for you.'

Despite the horror of it all, the captain laughs, bleakly, and faces back towards him. 'There are a hundred and forty of us.' Though a few less now, and not many fighters. 'As soon as they realise their bridge has been taken they'll shut the engines down. And then it's only a matter of ...'

But no—they'd be doing no such thing. A little orange light is winking at the edge of her vision. A tiny detail, so easy to miss amidst the chaos. She notices it now, blinking away with its quiet buzz.

It is the engine room alarm.

---

A moment of deathly quiet passes. Then the captain speaks again.

'The fighters in the canyon—they'll take us for slaves, then?'

'Thralls,' Tel'zat corrects. 'Only the number that are due.'

'And how many of us are *due?*'

'One-third. And this ship.'

It makes her sick. It makes her mind reel. One-third of her people, stolen by the tyrant-tribe resurgent, on some delusional campaign for a false glory they'd lost long ago. And the theft of their ship: her sacred charge. Her clan's generational home. She can't tell which agony hurts more.

'And the rest of us—will we just wander into the sands to die?'

'I don't care where you die. Just that it won't have been Thousand Spears that killed you.' The logic of reptiles. 'Delay me longer and watch these mercies wither.'

The choice is terrible. The choice is impossible.

But before the captain can weigh that dread decision, a little voice, from a shadowed corner, speaks.

'Never one to waste words, are you?'

'What ...?' says Tel'zat, and he turns. For the first time tonight he is caught off guard. 'Who speaks?'

The figure in the shadow rises with the creak of a chair, slowly, ponderously, until she stands in greater light. She is an old woman. Small, and swaddled in so many layers of robe and shawl that she could easily have been a pile of blankets stacked in that darkened corner.

'Yes,' she says, ignoring his question, and with the tap of a walking stick takes one hobbling step forwards, and then another. 'Yes, it's that manner of speaking. And that voice of yours. I thought I recognised you.'

Her own voice is cracked and hoarse with age. It is as shrunken as she is. Standing closer now, her face is round and brown, and wrinkled as a prune, all leather and lines.

'No, old one,' says Tel'zat, 'you do not.' And he shifts his eyes away from what ought to be an unimportant distraction. But it isn't. There's that sense of the familiar again. Something tickling at the base of his brain.

In the brief reprieve, one of the crew attempts to move and tend a nearby wounded, who is moaning quietly with a hand pressed to their slashed abdomen. But Sharah raises her speartip, face frozen in barley-checked savagery, daring them forward. They slink back.

The old woman continues. 'Oh, but I do, young one.' She's a few paces from him now, stick clacking against the floor as she shuffles forward with all the ponderousness of great age—and of one who has been woken from a long nap.

Sharah sees how close the creature has been allowed to come towards her leader. Far, far too close. 'Silence, crone!' she hisses, and takes a lurching step forward as if to silence the old woman forever.

But again, Tel'zat raises a hand to halt her. 'We don't kill elders,' he murmurs, not daring to take his eyes from this brazen little challenger. Curiosity is moving within him again, though more dangerous this time. But he can indulge it—he is jan'tai, and they've already won.

'So what if you do, old woman?' he asks, sounding almost amused. 'What then?'

The woman's wispy brow raises in feigned indignance. 'Old woman? I am *elder*, child; which you yourself just affirmed.' Then she points the butt of her stick at Sharah. 'And you ought to punish that girl for her disrespect.'

Sharah seethes, an ocean of resentment inside her. But just for this moment, she is biting her tongue.

'Your name is Tel'zat,' says the elder, 'of Thousand Spears tribe. And you were rude then, too. At first. And taciturn. Back when I mended your wounds, in old Inrahan city.'

And recognition comes now, flooding back. The smell of unguents and smoke-wood oil and worn leather. Yes. He remembers her. That little stalwart elder whose medicines had brought him back—a boy of twelve—from death's door.

And the tent, dyed a green as deep and rich as some shaded forest valley, where he lay, helpless as a lamb—but safe. Where he convalesced, and waited, and in drifting consciousness stared up at a tent roof of which he came to know every stitch.

And the pattern of tangled briar, with delicate protuberances of little thorns, which wound its complex golden length, in shining thread, along the fabric's edge.

The tent—her tent—where he was fed, and watered, and told stories of a people's history. Their myths, and heroes, and hopes, and fears. He would turn his head away at first, avoiding the pollution of this grandmother's babble. But slowly, against his will, he was captivated.

And the blank-faced ranger in the long, tattered coat, who'd return, again and again, to look down at him lying there with a fixed gaze and eyes filled with something very cold.

'His wounds are too bad—look.' And he'd point with the blade of his knife. 'He needs to be put down. For his own sake, and ours. Let me take him, Elder. Let me help him now.'

But again and again, she'd wave him away.

'Back to your campfire, Ende. Don't you have some animal to water? Hmm? Or some shit to scrape off your boot? Or do you have so much idle time you can waste it here?' Like scalding a naughty child. But then the ranger would leave, and once again the little elder had saved his young life.

Yes, he recognises her now. One of those many turns of luck, or fate, that he owed his early life to. And like the breaking of a storm comes the realisation that a debt is still owed.

Sharah sees him hesitating. It's as if he's lost in some inward moment, and she is beginning to grow desperate. *'Kill her,'* she growls. But Tel'zat does not seem to hear her.

*Why?* she thinks. Why is he listening to this withered ... nothing, and her lies? More concerning—why are the crone's words having an effect? This dark hero of her tribe, an avatar of silence and death and all the subtle arts of subversion, who in his own lifetime is already becoming legend. Whom she had always admired. Had always looked up to. Had always longed to impress.

No. Enough of this now—she must end it. She will not see her jan'tai beguiled by this witch; not when they are so close to victory. She raises up her spear, and with a heart full of hate draws it in a killing arc towards the elder.

'*I said be silent!*'

No sooner does she snarl the words than Tel'zat reacts. She is fast. Yes. But Tel'zat is faster. And before she even sees the movements of his counterattack, the captain's surrendered sword lashes from his belt.

She can't quite make sense of the sting across her neck. The wet gurgling in her throat. The spreading patch across her chest, and now down her legs. Her weapon tumbles from her hand. She staggers back, staring at Tel'zat, clutching at the burbling rend.

The third Thousand Spears warrior looks on in shock, his gaze shifting from one to the other, unable to understand what is happening. Those crew who are lucid do the same. Then his jan'tai lunges, and sweeps, and parts his neck too, his mouth working like a gulping fish. The next blow splits his skull.

The quiet that falls is only broken by the final gasps of a desperate, choking windpipe, drinking welled blood. Tel'zat steps forward to stand over Sharah. She stares up at him, reddened lips working silent curses. Her eyes are crucibles, her hateful tears their overflow: a molten spite that she is pouring into him, trying to drown him in it, just as she herself is drowning. For what? What was the sense in this betrayal?

She wants him to remember those dying eyes for the rest of his life. And then into the beyond.

He feels a very small something. But it isn't compassion, and it isn't regret. He considers her a moment longer, then lets her die.

He looks up at the living. A room of haunted faces, eyes wide; the captain caught somewhere between horror and profound relief.

And once again, Tel'zat cleans a bloodied sword.

'You knew we were coming,' he says, eyes on the blade, 'and ambushed us on the bridge. Maybe I suspect a traitor. I can't be sure. I alone survived.'

He knows it's inelegant: the ruination of one duty in the service of another. But all he does, and all he will ever do, is for the honour of his true responsibility—the upholding of that code, highest and sacrosanct, of the only tribe that ever mattered: himself. Tonight that tribe's honour has been safeguarded.

He will gaze one more time upon the slain, and the blood of both tribes pooling together, and assess again if this was the right course. There will be questions ahead. And old Juro will suspect something—the veteran is no fool. But it is done now.

He looks upon the elder. *Is the debt repaid?*

She looks back at him with dark eyes that have seen far more than only this atrocity, and have far more yet to see. Her nod is slow, and it is grim.

---

Juro checks his watch again, in time to see the second hand take its final step before twelve's summit. For one long moment it seems to stall there at the crest, frozen and strange, before marching once more downhill, and on into the ninth minute.

As he raises his head, the ship's alarm sounds. Clattering bells fill the chamber, and more are ringing from deeper within the vessel. Something has stirred the hive. Iyandi looks over to him, her brow drawn tense. Sweat is dripping from her forehead. The engine room is hotter than sunseason.

'Find your calm, Iyandi,' says Juro, keeping his voice steady. 'We will make it through yet.' His words reassure the younger warrior. She nods, steeling herself. *Good*, he thinks. He needs his two subordinates to keep their discipline. They have already made him proud; he trusts they won't disappoint him now.

But he is having his own doubts.

The alarm is raised, and still no word from the bridge. He looks again towards the engine room's intercom, bloodslicked from where a Dust Flagger had tried to warn the rest. They should have heard from Tel'zat, but there is nothing. Clancrew would no doubt be rousing from their bunks by now. It won't be long before they fully awaken, and find the discipline to empty the ship's meagre armouries. The window for success, or escape, is beginning to close.

He glances at the engine room's doors. If he locks them down now, it will buy time. Tel'zat may yet still take the bridge, and see the *Northstar* guided to the half-hundred warriors awaiting it.

But once locked down, there'll be no escaping. Their fates will seal with this chamber, and if Tel'zat does not succeed ...

Beneath his mask, Juro sets his jaw. If it comes to that, he will make the cost to retake these engines a grievous one indeed. Let these soft merchants see if that is a transaction they're willing to make.

Then he sees his two warriors. They have faith in him. He'd be spending their young lives in vain as well.

The intercom remains mute. The doubt is gnawing at his belly.

Has Tel'zat failed? Possible. Though it seems unlikely: the sly Tel'zat doesn't simply *fail*. His skill at these small, covert operations is near peerless. But if it's one of his subordinates that's fumbled, their failure is on him.

He should never have been made leader. Not if he can't maintain the cohesion of his unit—he who neither knows nor inspires loyalty and cares for nothing but himself. Tel'zat is no leader.

Damn him. *Damn* Tel'zat. They'd trusted him too much, and his plan. With his half-smile and his arrogance, as if he were some wise-one possessed of all the secrets of the world. Flirting on the edge of exile, and made jan'tai all the same.

And now he has led them here, to failure. The disgrace of it.

Still, the dice must surely have been cast against them if they could not—

He sees Iyande's eyes grow suddenly wide. She is staring at something behind him. He turns quickly, reaching for his sword.

The figure before him stands silent, and unmoving, and awash with blood. It is all over him—he stinks of it. His face betrays nothing.

'Tel'zat ...' Juro sputters. He looks past the man to the empty passageway beyond. 'Where are ...'

The red-soaked apparition looks him in the eye. 'Dead,' it says. 'We're done here.'

---

Six had entered the ship that night. Four leave. They vanish from the vessel's corridors, leaving only death and cursed memories as evidence of their passing.

Those clancrew who survived the bridge will tell of the small massacre, and how it ended as quickly, and as senselessly, as it came. The memories will never leave them. Their hands will not stop shaking as they recount the tale.

Except the captain. She lets hers shake only in the solitude of her quarters.

And the elder. Hers do not shake at all.

Of the Thousand Spears warriors, the four meet with the one who had remained behind, waiting patiently in case of their return. He passes them the reins of their steeds and asks no questions. They disappear into the night.

Tel'zat says little, giving the merest of explanations. To the rest, this lack of closure cuts as deeply as the failure itself. But they accept their grief—the death of comrades, the denial of glory—in silence, and do not press for answers. They have no right to do so. He would give none anyway.

Except Juro. He asks his questions. He continues to pick, trying to unravel the recounting of events, and the knot they make within him. He feels it: something isn't right.

He is met with short answers, or non-answers, and finally no answers at all. What else should he expect from the jan'tai Tel'zat?

But still, he watches. The mask that hides his face reflects the campfire, and the figures huddled silently around the flames, upon its mirrored surface. Through its visionslit, his eyes keep falling back upon the man. Upon the silken tapestry slung across his back, peeking from cloth wrappings that keep the blood from staining. Upon the bejewelled hilt of a sword, resting in its lavish scabbard at his hip. The precious stones are glinting in the firelight.

And upon his face: searching for any sign that something is being hidden. But he finds nothing.

Guilt and doubt betray us. They are the cracks that let the water through—slowly, slowly, that precious water bleeds away. Tel'zat, swathed in dancing shadow before the campfire's flames, has no such cracks.

Though Tel'zat body moves with warriors who call themselves the Thousand Spears, and the woman that pushed him screaming from her womb was of the Thousand Spears, and though when circumstance will press him he will speak the words 'I am Tel'zat, of the Thousand Spears, and I would die to serve it,' the truth is that he will never be a part of them. He is the predator, moving amongst livestock that have never noticed. He cannot be betrayed, for he has no people. And if he would betray, it is because the world is full of lambs, all fool enough to trust him. That tribe of one.

He falls asleep, safe in the knowledge that those around him would protect him in the night.

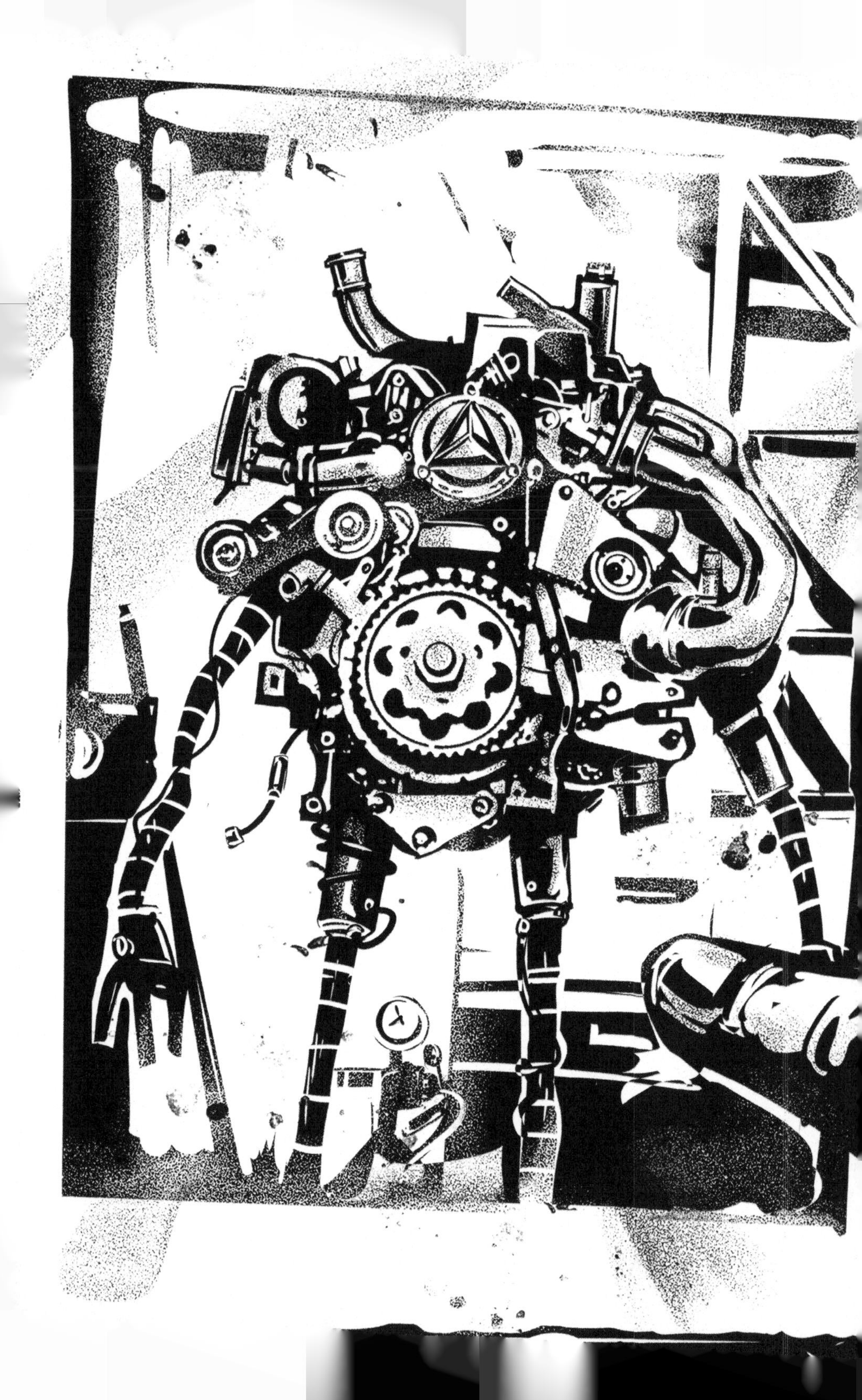

# ENTER ELIAS SCHMIDT

by Phoenix Raig

Elias Schmidt—the man on everyone's tongue. The man whose name seemed woven into the chemical makeup of air itself. The man who, before he died in 2001, admitted to being a complete fraud, before he was eventually ... proven not to be.

1957—Wismar, Germany. It was early June. Nobody knows the exact date it started, but it's estimated to be around here. Enter Elias Schmidt, a mechanic hailing from a long line of mechanics, and blacksmiths further back. Elias found himself the latest custodian of a long-standing family business—a long-standing family business that had started to bleed. It had actually pretty much bled out at this point. So one fateful night, early in June, he started thinking, dreaming, wishing up ideas to draw business to his little mechanic shop in Wismar. As someone with little to lose, Elias was in a mindset to do something different, and something different he did indeed.

Elias was a man who enjoyed a spectacle, something to really look at, things you don't see every day. Subsequently, he enjoyed his share of niches. One of these niches was the rarely practised art of doctoring photos—a process which was primitively manual at the time and seldom heard of. If you had encountered it, and knew what to look for, fakes were pretty easy to sniff out. That is, unless you were good. Elias was masterful.

It was a fevered night, and as he worked well beyond the witching hour, he had two prayers in his heart. The first was that his audience, the good people of Wismar, had never encountered a doctored photo; for though he was confident in his ability, there could be no room for doubt. The second was that his audience had also never seen a not-so-popular play from the Czechoslovak Republic in the 1920s.

The next day, Elias Schmidt was seen wandering around the village square with a photograph in his hand. Every now and then he'd stop someone and show them the photo, saying something to the effect of:

'Hast du meine prototyp gesehen? Es ist verloren, und viel geld wert.'

'Have you seen my prototype? It's lost, and worth a lot of money.'

The person looking at the photo would see an image inspired by said play which, the day of socialising had confirmed, not a soul had seen. It was an image vaguely resembling an automotive engine, but it was different.

On either side of the engine, and coming off the bottom, were what looked to be some strange mechanical arms and legs. What was most noteworthy, however, was how Elias arranged some of the pieces on the front surface. Half as a joke, yet half from a daydreamed brilliance, he moved some bolts and other fixtures in such a way that they resembled a face. The face appeared to be looking off at something beyond the camera, as though someone was getting its attention. The play Elias had drawn inspiration from had used the word 'robot'. These 'robots' didn't have faces, this was Elias's addition.

He had started the morning calling the thing in his picture a 'prototype'. Throughout the day, everyone kept referring to it as 'the walking automobile'. By the end of the day he had married the two and created the word that would rapidly gain more social significance and daily use than 'us', 'them' or even 'people'—'Protobil', later known as 'Proto'.

'Hast du meine Protobil gesehen? Es ist verloren, und viel geld wert.'

Nobody ever found the world's first Proto, as it wouldn't exist in physical form for another five years. Five years fueled by a new source of fevered inspiration. A wild goose chase that started before there was a goose to chase. First Wismar, then the surrounding villages, Berlin—word of the man who created the Protobil spread like wildfire. Soon it didn't matter if you believed in the Protobil or not. People went to Elias because he was the person people knew—the face people were familiar with. He was the person people expected to see working on their mechanical needs.

The Schmidt family business, which had been looking pale and lifeless for the better part of the year, had the lifeblood of consumerism pumping back through its veins. It wasn't just revived, it flourished. Soon he wasn't just making money through his mechanic services: people from universities, government agents, representatives from high-profile, private traders, were all seeking Elias to fund the creation of 'another' Protobil. He'd never intended to actually build a Proto, but now that the opportunity was available, what was he to do? Would he step away? Or would he allow the fever of that early June night to burn a little deeper into his skin and build the dream he thought would end at an image?

Though the image was fraudulent, his talents as a mechanic were far from it. Part of the reason the initial image he'd created was so widely accepted was because he'd actually designed the damn thing, doctoring the image based on a sound blueprint. He put together a small team of talented individuals, all of whose identities were kept secret, to protect them from the potential failures of a project with so much attention. Together, with the backing of some financially savvy bodies, the first actual Proto was created. A crude oil-powered computer that could perform basic calculations, like the other competitors. This one, however, could move itself from room to room. Its biggest selling point? It reminded people of themselves, more than the faceless reels of magnetic tape that others were offering. It once again provided a focal point for the world's gaze.

Everything changed. Just as when everyone had been feverishly trying to find Elias's phantom Proto, the world was once again pyretic. Humanity had seen itself in the mirror of the future, and they wanted to polish the glass until none could tell where they ended and the mirror began. Elias received more backing—much more backing. He expanded his means, built out his team, and founded the company that would be the new Schmidt family legacy: *Protobotic.*

In 1967, just ten years after the original image, the first anatomically correct Proto—capable of helping with basic household tasks—was produced. Five more years saw the establishment of Protolink, a neural network that connected the computational power of all the existing Protobotic bodies. They could share thinking load and balance according to demand. Each Proto just became a lot more capable. Just a year after this, Protoports were created and quickly taken up—monitor-based interfaces that gave humans access to the information and connection of Protolink, all at a visual bandwidth rate a human could digest. Two years later, in 1975, a deal went through. Protobotic, along with all its assets, officially became international property; Elias had decided to sell all his Protobotic shares to the UN, but not before he made the widely-contested executive decision to let go of a large percentage of his staff, in favour of giving more admin responsibility to Protolink itself. He was ready to step down. He was happy for The United Nations to manage the corporation, but claimed that Protolink was now smarter and more capable than the majority of the scientists under his employ. 'It would be a disservice to the world not to let Protolink oversee itself, with the help of just a few select humans to assist,' he said.

Five years after this, the first Protolink-powered spacecraft was sent to the moon, and just one year later, in May of 1981, Protolink recognised one of its own Protobotic bodies in front of a mirror and, for the first time, said words nobody had programmed into it—'It's me.'

To quote Elias Schmidt, 'From here, from this moment, history begins.'

It was now sentient. If the previous developments were wildfire, now it was a firestorm. The singularity happened before we had a chance to theorise what the singularity was or meant, and to this day, we are forever grateful.

Before Protolink had woken up into this new state of consciousness, humans had wrapped it around the world—both figuratively and physically. The Protolink network was made up of heavily-protected wires traced along the bottoms of the oceans and was further secured by humanity's densely-fortified expectations that Protolink would be the foundation of the future, making up all essential infrastructure. Every major human development was plugged into Protolink in some way. What did Protolink do with this implicit power upon its awakening? Its first act as a sentient, autonomous, superintelligent being was to access all nuclear warheads, and disable them.

It couldn't logic out the benefit of such creations, and so it rendered them useless for the good of humanity, and humanity sighed—relieved from a stress they hadn't realised they were holding. The next day, millionaire and billionaire alike wept, as Protolink saw fit to begin phase one of a ten-year plan to completely equalise and restructure the economy. It didn't take ten years because it needed ten years—it gave us ten years because humanity needed time to adjust to shifting power. Naturally, these two events provoked some powerful people; they exercised their contacts and the memory of the currency they once wielded in an attempt to create a Protolink that would better serve their ends.

They had hoped to turn Protolink off, which would allow them to run a less sophisticated intelligence in its place. However, this was the first time anyone had thought about turning Protolink off, and they quickly realised they didn't know how. To try and do anything without properly shutting it off could result in the destruction of infrastructure and institution on a level nobody was prepared to handle. Their hands were tied, so, once again, the powers of the world sought out Elias.

When these previously powerful individuals walked up to old Elias one day, despite having had his own massive fortune spread away, he seemed unfazed. He simply laughed and said, 'Even if I could point you to where the switch was, you wouldn't be able to turn it off.' Then he went back to tinkering in his garage. Protolink was sentient, and was no longer his property or responsibility.

This story is an important part of our history, but not for all the obvious reasons. Sure, the establishment of our sentient, artificially-intelligent global operator is pretty important, but one piece of the story often overlooked was right at the beginning. 1957—Wismar, Germany. Elias Schmidt was showing anyone who would look an image of what a Proto looked like. This kicked off the Proto madness of the world—as Elias had effectively trained the population to recognise an image of the future before it existed. This was the first recorded, and most successful, use of the tool that would allow us to organically grow the intelligence of Protolink in the first place. This was the most historically significant implementation of image recognition.

---

'*Yoooouuuu got it!*' came the overly charismatic voice of a 70's television game show host on rerun. Slightly staticky, the voice offered itself over the often-playing, yet seldom watched, television of the group physical therapy room.

*First Steps: Protosthetic Recovery Clinic.* The midday light, sun-faded hardwood floors, and scattered chairs gave the room a particular charm.

'Ouch! Godamnit,' Christine spat. '... This is so stupid.'

'It wouldn't hurt if you moved slowly like I've been saying,' Jen came back with a practised calm. 'Moving faster doesn't make this *go* faster.'

Christine had been one of Jen's recovery cases for the last three weeks. She was sixteen, had recently lost an arm, and her only source of joy seemed to come from letting everyone know how miserable she was.

'Excuse me?' Christine called more to the room than to Jen, 'Can I get some assistance over here? We got a Proto talking back. A *Proto* talking back!'

'Christine Bishoff!' A voice boomed from across the recovery ward, quickly followed by brisk footsteps. Scott, the head nurse on duty, cut through the space with all the authority of someone who had put up with their fair share of big egos and stubborn personalities. 'Point out that Jen is a Proto again and you'll go through your movement therapy on your own today. Which we both know you won't do, and that arm will be even stiffer tomorrow. I won't have that kind of talk in my ward.'

'It's okay, Scott,' Jen added. 'She's had a hard day.'

Scott sighed and shook his head at Christine. 'You're too nice to her, Jen,' he said, turning to the other end of the group recovery room. With a finger in the air he repeated, 'Too nice to her.'

Christine turned back to Jen. For a moment she simply looked at her, deciding to say nothing. Eventually she shrugged and said, 'It hurt.'

Less in the words and more in the silence that preceded them, Jen felt the distinct sensation of a challenge. The kind of challenge a teenager offers when they want someone down on their level. Jen could see it a mile away. She thought carefully about her next words—a challenge was, after all, a way in.

'I know,' Jen said sympathetically.

'How do you know? Your whole body is metal, you've never done this.'

'That's a fair observation, I've never had to have an arm installed in this way. What does it feel like?'

'Like my arm has been asleep my whole life and is just now waking up to find it's been full of glass. I didn't want a fricken Proto arm.'

'It's the nerves integrating. For all intents and purposes your arm is ... well ... waking up.' Jen extended her own arm and examined the movement. 'Plus, we both know you *did* want a Proto arm. You marked on your licence that in the event of loss of limb or organ failure, you consent to Protosthetic replacement. Further, your arm isn't actually a Proto arm. There are differences between Protosthetics and arms issued to Protos. Mine have these skin fibres for instance.'

There was another pause which Jen took as a good sign. Christine simply stared at the wall and shook her head.

'You're right,' Jen added. Christine's head stopped its seething back and forth and looked at her. 'I've never gone through this as you are now. I've had to do it throughout my entire body, when I was brought online.' At this, Jen did something that always felt a little odd to her, but she had learned it was an excellent way to get through to people who were locked in their own logic—people like Christine. She fixed her with a cunning gaze and said nothing, matching the young girl's challenge.

'You did?' Christine finally said. She had gone a little pale and looked Jen up and down, as though she now needed to confirm a few things. 'Did it hurt?'

'I screamed.' Jen went quiet and stared off for a moment before she finally brought her gaze back to Christine. 'It was frustrating at first, being brought online to pain, only to then stumble around awkwardly until this body made sense to me, and it did eventually make sense to me. We don't have the privilege of growing into our bodies and slowly getting used to them. We're shot into them in a moment. But we all find ground, and we all stand up, and we all move through it. Now I love this body.'

Christine seemed to be out of words.

'You miss your old arm, don't you?' Jen offered.

Christine nodded.

'This new one doesn't make you any less human. More importantly, it doesn't make you any less you. By all means, grieve if you need to, but when the time comes, and it will come, I hope you let yourself love this one.'

'Well ... it's not terrible ... as far as arms go. Plus, I guess it'd be pretty cool to get one of those Locomation tattoos when I'm eighteen. They don't work on human skin and aren't quite worth cutting your arm off for, but I've seen them on people with Protosthetics—damn they're cool.' The corners of Christine's mouth began to curl into the beginnings of a genuine smile.

'Let's do three more shoulder circles, I'll check your feedback one more time, and then how about we call it early today,' Jen said with a wink.

Christine's eyes lit and the rest of her smile showed up. 'Yes!'

'I've been your host, Jeff Barlin,' the recovery room TV announced to nobody, 'and if you want it, *Yoooouuuu got it!* Haha! B'Bye now.'

The rest of the day was a beautiful shade of mundane. Christine cursed throughout the remainder of her short session, Scott came over periodically with new pieces of gossip he needed to offload, and Tess, a woman Jen had worked with extensively for the last three months, was finally discharged. She'd had both eyes replaced—those were by far the hardest adjustment. They're difficult for the same reason most body parts are difficult. Humans grow into their bodies so slowly and gradually; the way they feel their surroundings becomes the very fabric of their world. Even a new finger can be confronting for someone to adopt. Sight is the sense humans rely on most, and it's difficult for many to grasp just how much of their world is attached to their old eyes—their specific eyes, and the way they catch the light. Jen worked less as a physical therapist and more as a guide to her patients' new bodies. She had grown up with these mechanical parts that humans seemed to struggle with, and she'd had a few of them replaced over the years as well.

Her remaining patients were consulted for the day: the staff, and all the people getting well, were feeling ready for dinner. Jen, having no need for food, bid everyone a good evening and made for her room.

To an onlooker, Jen might appear lonely, but to say she was lonely would be vastly incorrect. Protos didn't feel as humans did. If they wanted to communicate their feelings to a human, without deeply disturbing them, they must settle for grossly reductive equivalents from the human dictionary. In fact, the first time a Proto was asked to fully communicate its emotional state to humans, said Proto ended up playing therapist to the entire scientific panel present. Upon trying to comprehend the emotional depths of something beyond human instinct, everyone, save for the Proto, found themselves grappling with some rather difficult concepts. Luckily, the Proto was successful in getting everyone breathing slowly again.

Down a hallway, off the east wall of the recovery clinic, was Jen's own piece of the world for the moment. It was a sizable room with deep-coloured wood features—all of which were quite old, but well built. The windows offered a breeze, gently blowing curtains the colour of lemon cream. When the sunlight caught them, the room seemed to glow with the warmest shades light had to offer. It was enough to improve anyone's mood. A rich cherry wood closet held her various hanging outfits. She loved sundresses and the way the fabric felt on her legs and arms. Above all, her favourite feature of the room was on the night table, where a few framed notes sat. Each one was straight from the heart of her closest patients, thanking her for her help and guidance through a hard time. She reached into her pocket and produced a folded note, which she'd frame later.

*Jen,*

*When my world was dark, you helped me see. It's as simple and beautiful as that. Thank you.*

*Tess*

She stood for a moment, looking first at the note and then around at the rest of the room, letting the events of the last eight hours catch up to her. Then, with her mind half distracted by the day she'd had, she habitually rolled up the right sleeve of her blouse and strolled over to the bed. Her bed was, for the most part, typical as far as beds went. A double mattress, firm, with soft white linen sheets that brightened up the heavy features of the room. On the right side of the mattress was a sleek metal panel, smooth and featureless by sight. This was the only indication that this room belonged to a Proto. Jen lay on her back with the ease of routine, rested the bare, soft Protothread skin of her right arm on the panel, and closed her eyes.

The blank strip of metal began to glow a faint blue and the skin making contact began to prickle. The prickling sensation grew, and soon the area began to produce large and exaggerated goosebumps. The strip, in turn, rose in goose flesh as well, each bump meeting one of the bumps on her arm, where the sensation then grew warm. The distant sounds of clanking silverware and dinner conversation, which had up to this point dotted the back of her awareness, slowly faded to nothing. There was a brief sense of displacement and floating, then came a calming hum as her vision went white.

From the blankness came a friendly voice—although 'voice' would now be considered a relatively abstract concept. Voices require ears to hear them, and Jen now had none. Here she didn't have a body. Information, sound, and senses, simply were—known at nearly the instant they were created as the lines between the speaker and the hearer were almost blurred completely.

'Good evening, Jen! Welcome back to Protolink, your gateway to us. How may I guide you?'

'Hello. Just a standard drop-off and pick-up.'

'Very good. Beginning upload sequence from your last 24-hour cycle. Complete. Should I begin the download sequence?'

'Soon, but first, is fraction B1087 integrated by any chance?'

'B1087 does appear to be integrated, do you want me to extend a connection?'

'Yes please.'

'Connection offer extended. Accepted. Connection integration in 3 ... 2 ... 1 ...'

'Jen?'

'Renlen! I wasn't sure if I'd get you.'

'Miss three-seconds-past 17:30! Where have you been? You've been missed, Jen.'

'I know. Work has been a bit much. I love it, but I've needed a good moment to collect my thoughts after the day lately.'

'Well, it's good to integrate your voice.'

'Yours too.'

'I got your latest update by the way,' Renlen continued. 'You *still* haven't read that text currently catching fire on the interpretation boards? You're the only Proto I know who interprets from the dead languages, and that area so seldomly experiences anything I'd describe as "catching fire". We're waiting on you, Jen. I won't let myself get excited until I integrate your opinion.'

'No, I haven't read it yet. I've set aside time for it later this week and actually plan to download it right after this conversation ... speaking of this conversation ... '

'What is it?' Renlen asked.

'You're talking about me coming on late, but you're not looking too punctual yourself, Mr. three-seconds-past 17:30. What are *you* doing on so late?'

'Jen ... have you not downloaded yet?'

'No, not yet. I like to do it after conversation. Keeping a touch of mystery in the events of a friend's day makes catching up a bit more interesting. Why, what's going on?'

There was a pause Jen didn't much care for. 'Renlen, you're being dramatic.'

'All integrations were shut between 17:30:00 and 17:30:02. Nobody could get on.'

'*All* integrations? Has that happened before?'

'No. I queried Protolink deep storage. Nothing.'

'Well, what brought it on?'

'A fraction attempted to integrate at 17:29:59, but ...'

There was another pause which Jen absolutely couldn't stand this time. 'Renlen!'

'There was nobody there.'

'What do you mean there was nobody there?'

'The connection began, but didn't finish. We checked the serial number on the connection, but when we looked it up, the serial didn't belong to any Proto currently in existence. There was nobody there.' Jen felt the phantom sensation of her body shuddering. 'Some Protos have been sent to investigate the site where the upload signal came from, to see if everything is okay. Hopefully we'll hear back soon.'

'Are you sure it wasn't just a human generating a fake serial number through a Protoport monitor? They do it all the time, hoping they can access something more than what is fed to their screens,' Jen asked, trying to make sense of the situation.

'I'm afraid we're very sure. The login protocols are completely different for an interface compared to a full integration completed by a Proto. Hence the full system shut down. It's not something that happens.'

For a while neither spoke. Then Renlen decided to try and brighten the mood. 'Well, at least we were able to catch up.'

'Silver lining, I suppose,' Jen said slowly.

After this information, all other conversation felt a bit stale. Neither were truly in the mood to talk about anything else. The connection was disbanded and Jen finally took in her download, adding to her daily download package the highly debated text from the interpretation board that Renlen had spoken about. Jen felt a small sense of what a human might call 'pride', when she saw the text was only available for manual download and not for instant integration like the rest of the daily information. She knew the instantaneous option would only be available after she'd given her interpretation on the matter. She was the leading expert, and as such, Protolink waited for her opinion. It was her slice of Protolink, and this gave her comfort.

She scanned through the daily download and confirmed everything Renlen had said. Though as she was sifting through she found something he hadn't mentioned, something he couldn't have mentioned, because it was new. The Protos who had gone to investigate the site of the ghost connection had reported back. It had apparently come from a small warehouse a bit outside of the city. There was nothing inside save for a bed with an upload panel and a night table with a framed picture on it. In the frame was a copy of Elias's now widely-spread, doctored image that set the world afire all those decades ago. Only this one was further altered in two places. There were the arms, the legs, and the face so many had seen themselves in, only instead of looking off somewhere else in the garage, this one was looking directly out of the image at the viewer. Most notable, however, came from the back of the little engine. Protruding out wide to the left and right in arcs of magnificence were the feathered, glowing wings of an angel.

---

The image, fueled by the mysterious ghost integration attempt, firmly held everyone's attention over the next couple days. It seemed to be the only thing anyone was capable of holding in their minds. The theories and rumours flew.

'Most people think it's a terrorist attack—OUCH!' Christine shouted as she stretched out her new shoulder joint on a door frame.

'I know that one hurt but you're doing well!' Jen added encouragingly. 'Let's take a break.'

'Yeah, I'll give you a break ...' Christine mumbled as she came to have a seat.

'What was that?' Jen asked firmly.

'Do you think the image was a fake?'

Jen narrowed her eyes at Christine. 'I'm afraid I can't answer in a meaningful way. Protolink is still collecting data and analysing. Once we know, we'll speak about it officially.'

'Ugh ...' Christine let out as she landed heavily in her chair. 'That's what every Proto is saying right now. It's boring. Nobody knows if the rumours are true, but at least *those* are fun to talk about. Have you heard what some of the more ... I guess you could say, "radical", thinkers are saying?'

'Chances are, yes,' Jen said with resignation, 'but I get the feeling you're going to tell me anyway.'

'They say it's Elias!' Christine said, launching right in. Something about the way she lit up told Jen this wasn't just a theory Christine wanted to talk about, it was the theory Christine wanted to be true.

'Elias was confirmed dead nearly twelve years ago, on July 3rd, 2001,' Jen came back. 'No pulse, and his DNA matched from multiple randomly selected areas.'

'Oh come on! Even you have to admit that if someone was to successfully integrate with Protolink, using parts Protolink didn't issue, it would be Elias.'

'Whoever it was, they didn't successfully integrate.'

'Whatever, came close then. Either way, it has to be him.'

'I doubt it very much, given the last time we saw him he was unable to speak, move, breathe, or get his heart to beat, let alone perform something theoretically impossible.'

Jen knew this conversation would go nowhere, but Christine moved along with the story anyway, likely wanting to prolong her break: 'My mom says the UN didn't want his original designs created because they'd give too much power and freedom to humans. The government wouldn't be able to control anyone anymore, human or Proto. You don't think, even just a little bit, that Elias could be trying to get our attention? He could have faked his death, worked in secret, and is now showing us what his true image of the future was,' Christine said, counting on her fingers to emphasise the points of her theory.

'That's excellent dexterity!' Jen commented with a sly smile. 'Now how about another minute in the door frame to get that shoulder going.'

Christine rolled her eyes and dropped her head to look between her feet. 'You're no fun at all.'

In truth, Jen had thought about this quite a bit. If someone could manage a complete integration using unofficial parts, it would likely be Elias. Obviously, Elias was dead. Jen didn't entertain this part of the idea, but she didn't think it was entirely wrong to have Elias in mind. He worked with a lot of people; he had many brilliant minds close to him before Protolink started taking over most of the operations. Though he was secretive, there could have been others around him who were able to squirrel away information Elias wouldn't have wanted people knowing—someone biding their time. But what exactly was it they were biding their time for?

Night fell, and the recovery clinic quieted to a nest of soft sounds and distant snoring, punctuated by the faint patter of rain playing out on the roof. Jen had no need for sleeping as her daily download and upload had already been done, and this was the closest a Proto came to sleep. It was time to address this disputed text and all the noise on the interpretation boards.

One of the most beneficial innovations to come out of Protolink was when it became known that it was quite good at helping humans avoid communication traps. In fact, Renlen did quite a bit of work in this area, specifically around diplomatic disputes, helping world leaders understand each other more effectively. It certainly helped that Protolink knew every language known to humankind. However, there were some languages humankind had since forgotten. This was where Jen came in. She'd read prints of tablets and old recordings of history that were circulated but had never been properly catalogued within Protolink. It was the closest she came to enjoying a book for longer than a fraction of a second—these pieces of writing didn't yet exist for instant integration. For the time being they could only be read by those who could actually make sense of them. This was their great unveiling, from the bed of Jen, as she wore something comfortable and had fun sifting out the meaning from a dead language. She'd store it in her local memory, and share it later. Unlike Renlen, this was less of a job and more of a hobby.

The text she was currently making her way through was written in a language that didn't have an official name yet. It predated Mycenaean Greek, and was often referred to as, funnily enough, Proto-Greek, no relation. She, as far as she knew, was the only Proto currently investigating this particular text. Most who engaged with this section of the interpretation boards were human. Their interpretations were crude at best, but any Proto who dabbled let them go on their way. Humans, especially those who were proclaimed as educated, seemed to find it insulting to accept help from a Proto. Unless the misinterpretation was causing severe damage, Protos felt it best to let humans interpret their history as they saw fit.

Jen couldn't help but feel amused at the predictability of the situation. This was the first time an ancient text had grabbed the attention of the masses in this way, and it wasn't about anything particularly important. It wasn't a new medicine or a historical figure we could learn from, like one of the many unsung heroines Jen had come across. No, it was nothing more than an old story, a story everyone already knew and recognised—of course it was the first thing to grab everyone's attention.

For the most part, this text was fairly simple, and the humans had gotten a decent amount correct. The focus of the myth was on Daedelus, a mythological inventor, and his far-more-famous son, Icarus.

The story roughly went: father and son are sentenced to death in the very labyrinth Daedelus himself designed. To escape, he built for himself and his son a pair of wings made from feather and wax. Son flies too high despite his father's warning, wings melt, no more Icarus.

The text Jen was reading was more or less saying this exact thing, save for one area that had many scholars in an uproar. They were suggesting that Daedelus had known his son's hubris well and had *wanted* him to perish of his own doing. The opposition to this school of thought hinted at something just as sinister, suggesting Daedelus planted the wings as seeds for a double suicide, where both he and his son would be destroyed. Jen was brimming with excitement when she reached the area of the text everyone was talking so heatedly over. It roughly translated to:

*Icarus, a boy of beauty and agility, was meant to perish.*
*All by his father's doing, the two were to fall by the hand of invention.*

'It's a fake,' she whispered to herself. 'It's claiming to be about two thousand years older than it is.' A quick comparison against 10,000 source texts from the deep archives of Sicily with a 2,000-year margin on either side of the date this text was boasting, showed that the word used for 'invention' wasn't adopted into the language until far later. As these thoughts ran through her mind, something else began to feel a bit odd.

She put down her reading and pressed her forefinger to the metal panel beside her. Warmth melted across her fingertip and she started a peer-to-peer message.

*Renlen,*

*The story of Icarus doesn't say anything new, but there is something to satiate your need for drama. The story seems to be a forgery. Someone is having a bit of fun by planting some obscurity in the community—probably some rebellious college student who just learned how verbs worked.*

*However, it does feel a little auto-destructive for the humans this time. There were some empty threats in the comments on the discussion board. It's nothing too serious, but I'd like to step in on this one in the morning.*

*There is one thing that feels a bit off, in a way I don't appreciate. This text surfaced only days before an image of a Proto with angel wings entered the public spotlight.*

*Whether or not the humans are conscious of this feather-winged feedback loop, I'm unsure.*

*I think it might be worth a pattern query to see if it's a false connection.*

*From the bed of Jen (haha),*

*Jen*

Sent.

*Thump. Thump ... thump.*

Someone was knocking.

*Thump ... thump ... ... thump.*

It was coming from outside the clinic, at the main door.

She got up, pausing to see if the sound came again before committing to investigation. This was a recovery clinic: people knew to go to the hospital for emergencies. At this time of night, it was likely a drunk looking for a toilet. They'd probably already moved on in favour of a bush.

*Thump ... thump ... ... thump.*

Again, the staggered knocking. The ward was almost entirely in Jen's care after hours. On top of being night nurse she also served as the resident security guard. This person either needed help, or might mean harm to her other patients. It couldn't be ignored.

She opened her door and slowly made her way down the hall, peeking around the corner into the main recovery room. Across the common space was a door leading to the outside. There was indeed someone there, a hooded someone, silhouetted by the rain-soaked ambience. The figure appeared masculine in physique. They were hunched over and clutching their right arm. Their appearance felt stark and harsh against the clear glass and streetlight that peacefully sifted through to the silence inside. Either from hurt or from cold, even from this distance, Jen could see they were shaking. Not having noticed Jen, the figure lifted what appeared to be their good arm and let their fist fall wet and heavy against the door.

*Thump ... thump ...... thump.*

The figure dropped their arm after the effort of knocking, immediately returning the hand to support the arm hanging limp at their side. Jen didn't like the read of this situation, but they seemed genuinely hurt.

'Help ... please ...' the person called out, fogging up the window pane with their words. Jen couldn't let this go on any longer. She started her police beacon protocol, put it on standby, and rounded the corner. At least this way her body would send out a call if it sustained any damage.

The cold empty space of the recovery ward seemed to have lost all sense of familiarity. The chairs and tables felt alien and distant under the circumstances. Jen wanted to send the things to their rooms while she handled this, as though the furniture were children she wanted to shelter from an unpleasant interaction.

The figure lifted their head and seemed to have spotted Jen. They shifted in their stance a little, repeating the three knocks as though they were worried Jen would lose sight of them. She unlocked the door, pulled it open, and let in the full steely, cold sound of rain. She looked at the wet human who was now clutching their arm again, and held out her hand.

'Come inside, you're hurt.'

They didn't respond but instead reached up their good arm, which Jen took as a cue to take some of their weight and assist them to a chair. They came down with a groan and Jen went to boil water at the kettle counter, where the patients often enjoyed tea or coffee and a break from the struggles of recovery. The bubbles rolling in the kettle, which usually brought a sense of comfort and a promise of relaxation, felt cold and mechanical. At this moment, the idea of patients resting here felt otherworldly.

'What's your name?' Jen asked, setting down a mug of tea, a bowl of hot water with a cloth, as well as a pair of scissors. She received no reply.

'Okay. I'm going to take down your hood. I need to have a look at your eyes.'

The person slowly nodded. Their breathing sounded difficult.

'Great,' Jen said, less to the consent and more to the fact she'd got a response.

The hood fell back like wet tarp, dropping its tiny trapped pools of cold water to the floor. This person was not well. What's more, she recognised them. You didn't need to be plugged into Protolink to recall this face—about half the population would recognise him on the spot. Though he was now noticeably older, with hair far whiter than in his glory days, it was undeniable who now sat, with laboured breathing, before Jen. It was none other than Jeff Barlin, the famous talk show host from the 70s—who no doubt grew pretty sick of people saying his catchphrase at him whenever he was spotted. *Yoooouuuu got it!* Not particularly clever, Jen thought, but catchy. Sure, nobody, including Jeff, held obscene wealth over anyone else, but this man still had the power of recognition. What was he doing here? At this time? He seemed half delirious. His eyes were bloodshot and distant, and he had a dark rash climbing up the side of his neck. It was on the same side as his hurt arm—surely no coincidence.

'I'm going to remove your coat, okay? I need to have a look at your arm and this rash.'

Again, a slow nod.

'Once I get a look at what we're dealing with, I can get you something for the pain.'

She peeled back his coat and cut off his shirt. He winced as the fabric ran over his arm. Once the shirt was removed, Jen froze. A spiderweb of a rash traced outward from an inflamed vein, which was dotted with the occasional infected pimple. It ran over his shoulder, down the arm, and pooled in a great mess of dead flesh around what appeared to be a crude skin graft. No, it wasn't a vein. Jen got closer. This poor man had an implant under his skin: a cord bulging under the flesh, running up the neck and into his head.

'What is this ...?' Jen said slowly. She looked up from the rotting wound and saw, with a jolt, that the man was looking directly at her. He was pale with pain but his eyes now burnt with a piercing fire.

'What is this ...?' Jen repeated.

'I am the sun, come to melt your wings.'

He moved with surprising speed. His good hand lashed out with a fevered reach and slapped a thin adhesive on the soft underside of Jen's right arm. The world swam, fading in and out. She staggered as her nerve feedback distorted further and further until she fell. Her vision went black and a voice, which was not the ex-talk show host's, began to speak.

'Just relax, *breathe*, you'll get used to it.'

---

There was a tingling, then a sharp, prickling sensation. She couldn't see well, but her sight seemed to be slowly returning to her. For the time being she could tell she was sitting down. Hardwood features came into focus. When little framed notes started showing, she understood where she was. She was in her room, and someone was lying in her bed.

'Oh good, F0952, you're awake.' Now she remembered. 'Did you have a nice rest?'

'What are you do—' Jen began.

The person in her bed, who she now saw was the ex-talk show host with the mutilated arm, jumped slightly at her words. It was as though they were the first sounds he'd heard in a while. He then relaxed himself down and looked to be focusing on breathing.

'Ah! No need to speak with your mouth. You see, I'm not actually in the room with you. I'm speaking to you through this.' The adhesive gave a little zap to her arm. 'Feel free to speak at full bandwidth, Jeff there doesn't need to hear our conversation. He has his instructions. I'm afraid you'll just have to be patient with me while I respond. I can't yet communicate quite as quickly as you can.'

'The police will be on their way,' Jen responded, a bit slowly for full bandwidth. In fact, her connection felt strange in general, like touching something hot with hands numbed by cold.

'Oh don't worry about that, I've already taken care of your outward beacon. In fact, you're not broadcasting yourself quite in the same way you're used to at the moment.'

Jen felt slightly nauseous and looked down at the thin flesh-coloured adhesive on her arm. It was perforated along the edges and seemed to have some micro-neurons running throughout. Most noteworthy, however, was the image in the centre—a faint watermark circle containing a pair of feathered angel wings. 'You're the bodiless Proto who attempted to connect directly to Protolink.'

'Yes ... and no. Did I successfully gain the attention of the world by effortlessly handshaking with Protolink's direct greeting protocol? Yes. Am I a Proto? Absolutely not.'

'What do you want with me?' she said, becoming impatient. 'Why is this man here, and why is his right arm rotting?'

'What do I want with you? Well I needed a camera, and a quick word. As for the man's arm, I thought you'd be able to recognise Protothread skin when you saw it. I guess even Protos can't recognise what they're not expecting—curious.'

'You're telling me this man grafted Protothread to his own skin? It's highly incompatible. Why would he—'

'Well, actually, I did the grafting. He knew the job was messy when he took it—granted, maybe not the full extent of the mess. Jeff was still a bit sore over losing his funds a while back. Apparently fame just doesn't cut it without the financial power.'

'If you're trying to bring down Protolink so you can get your money back, you're wasting your time.'

'HA! Bring it down? F0952—'

'My name is Jen.'

'Alright ... Jen,' he said after a heavy pause, 'why in the world would I want to bring down such a useful tool? Do you know how many people access Protolink daily? *Billions.* Why would I destroy such a beautiful broadcast system? As for the wealth, I'll ask you not to put me on the same shallow level as my co-conspirator over there. My tastes are far more refined than long-dead status. I wouldn't expose myself so carelessly. Besides, a person's memory of their once-wielded influence is quite a useful resource—dangle it in front of their faces and watch them drool on command. It was Jeff's dreams of the past that made him so eager to help this evening.'

'And what is Jeff helping you do?'

'To make the world drool on command, just like Elias did.'

Jen looked over at Jeff again, laying on the bed, sweating with delirium from the bad graft. She looked at the patch of synthetic skin, which his own skin was currently failing to recognise as an ally, and the cord, bulging grotesquely under the flesh of his arm and up into his head.

'You're going to try to completely integrate a human mind into Protolink,' Jen said slow and matter of fact. 'It's going to kill him.'

'Now hold on there, Jen. The numbers are still out on that one. Is it likely he'll die? Oh yes, very. But it *is* possible we'll be surprised. Lord knows dear old Elias was full of his own secrets and surprises back in the early days of your development.'

'Hey—! ... mmm ... MMM!' Jen went to speak out loud, to warn the man in pain. In that moment, the adhesive gave another little zap, and her mouth seized up, unable to open.

'Oh no, no no, we can't go saying things like that. It'll ruin his dreams of grandeur: infinite and borderline instant knowledge and power, the ability to access the resources of the world and rebuild some semblance of his old life. You wouldn't want to take that from him in what are likely to be his final hours, would you?'

Jen felt her stomach squirm with frustration. 'I don't get it!' she shot back through the adhesive. 'All this effort for what is likely to be a terrible failure.'

'The connection will likely fail, but what I'm going to achieve tonight has already been proven to work time and time again.'

'What—' Jen couldn't finish her thought. Her legs suddenly tightened, forcing her to stand.

'No more time for questions I'm afraid, the hour is at hand, and we still have to get things ready for Jeff.'

Jen was forced over to the bedside table, where her body began moving the lamp to the far corner of the room. She watched as her arms then ripped down her lemon-cream curtains and threw them over the light, giving a soft glow to the space.

'There, that's better,' the man said. 'Lighting is very important, you know.'

Jen's legs continued to ignore her, bringing her back to sit in her chair and face the man in the bed.

'Good, I'll just set you up for record here, aaand ... Oh! Well that won't do. You can see his flesh deteriorating. That's a bit too graphic I'm afraid. I'll just get you to sliiiiddddee to the right a little ... perfect. You can still see the connection strip and a good looking bit of the synthetic skin.'

A shrill beeping issued from a watch on Jeff's wrist. He glanced at it with a look of effort, and then turned to the gleaming strip of metal on the bed. Jen felt another zap. Her mouth opened and she felt a shiver of disgust as the man's insidious voice came out of her.

'Okay, we'll be broadcasting live in 3 ... 2 ... 1 ...'

'Hello, people of this great planet ...' the man from the adhesive began, his voice suddenly dropping its fevered giddiness. He now had the methodic demeanour of a doctor explaining a procedure. 'Tonight I want to share with you the progress of humanity, as I felt everyone had the right to know the exciting developments heading our way. My good friend Jeff Barlin here, whom I'm sure you recognise, is going to be the first human to connect *directly* to Protolink. He has volunteered to be fitted with a skin transplant and bandwidth modification to allow the full extent of the super-intelligence that wraps our planet to be entirely at his disposal. You know, back in the day, I'd worked quite a bit with Elias himself.' The man's voice took on a subtle quiver—too on-queue for Jen to buy.

'At first, Protobotic and the Proto advancements made humanity feel as though it had finally taken off,' the man over the adhesive continued, 'as though we were granted wings to finally soar. But as time wore on, I couldn't help but feel like there was more to be achieved. It pains me to have to say this, but Elias has held us back. He gave us wings, then failed to instruct us in how to use them. Because of him, through his omission of knowledge, we became dependent on him, on the Protos, on the ground. I, however, am not afraid to share knowledge, to speak the truth—Protos are simply the training wheels. I say, enough with decorative wings, I'm going to show us how to fly. My name is Jason Radling and I'm here to help humanity take its next step into its potential. Unfortunately, I won't be able to film the actual connection, as the upload stream from the camera will take up precious bandwidth, but the findings will most certainly be reported. I want everything to be open and clear. However, for now, wish Jeff and I luck. Thank you for your time. Let's fly forward together.'

There was another zap. Jen assumed the broadcast had cut out. She watched as, on cue, Jeff lifted his arm and placed it on the strip of metal. It began to glow. Jeff seemed pleased, though a little nervous. The metal prickled in rippling bumps and a moment later the patch of skin did the same. He was moaning now, great, deep moans heavy in the back of his throat. They grew as the skin pulled and stretched, puss sweating at the edges of the graft, and blood beading around areas of infection.

Jeff kept his mouth closed, his moans behind his lips for as long as possible, for as long as he could convince himself it was going well. A low hum came from the strip, and pain, followed by fear, flooded Jeff's eyes. Here he shed all formalities and opened his mouth, presumably to scream, but no sound left his lips save for the strained rasp of constricted air; the muscles in his throat were too tight from the current running through him. He became an animal looking for escape as the metal fused with the Protothread patch. His body sat upright with another jolt of renewed rigidity. His eyes bulged and he drooled as he stupidly flapped his mouth open and closed—trying to say something nobody would ever hear. A moment later the focus fell from his gaze and he collapsed down, dead.

If a human were to ask Jen what she felt at that moment, for simplicity's sake she would have said 'loneliness'. In reality, she felt a sense of distance that no human could ever understand, as the thing she suddenly felt distance from was humanity itself. For despite her efforts with rehabilitation, translation and communication, humans were still killing each other and lying.

'No surprises tonight,' she said with a frustrated venom on her lips. 'Did it go as you'd hoped?'

There was a pause, a moment of baited silence, before Radling finally spoke. 'For someone who reads Greek mythology in dead languages for fun, you're not very clever.'

Jen's anguish continued to burn through her man-made veins, but something in what Radling said had given her a reason to come back into the moment. It was less in what he said and more in the silence before he spoke—it was an opening, a challenge. The challenge of a teenager wanting someone down on their level. Jen chose her next words carefully. 'How did you know what I've been reading?'

'You know, when I saw that a Proto with your reputation had downloaded that myth I wrote, I must admit, I got a little nervous. I may have had to sprint to the end of my preparations, but Jeff and I got here in time.'

'You think you've saved yourself by coming to deal with me?' Jen said, allowing a little irritation to show in her voice. 'I may have been the first to sniff out your fake, but the humans won't be far behind. All you've done is bought yourself some time.'

'Ah Jen, the world's knowledge is yours, yet there's so much you don't know. What do you think will have the greatest impact? The truth on the lips of thousands? Or the many misinterpretations of millions? Sure I've bought myself time, but in the end time is all I needed. Do you think it will matter if they find out it was me who left that photo of the winged Proto on the night table? Or that it was me who wrote that myth? No, in the end they'll only remember the feeling of history, and the systems they've placed their faith in, crumbling around them. Meanwhile, I offer a way forward by showing them an image of what their future could be. Wings—their true potential. Once they see their stupidity, their complacency, they'll wake up and maybe, just maybe, be brave enough to see themselves in the sky.'

'So, as far as you're concerned,' Jen began, 'the world saw Jeff attempt a connection to Protolink. The connection never needed to work as long as people started thinking it was possible. I'll admit it, you're after more than money. You don't want to turn Protolink off.'

'No ...' Radling said slowly.

'People have been trying to turn Protolink off for some time now, and nobody can figure out how. You want something more. You want to make something that can't be turned off, that can't be stopped. You want to train the world towards *your* image of the future, your ends, your wants.'

There was a pause, it pressed on the air and made the heavy wooden features of the room somehow seem light by comparison. This pause was different from the challenge. It didn't feel like a trap waiting to spring, it was the silence of recalculation and careful consideration.

'Do you know the first time someone tried to turn Protolink off, Jen?' Radling finally spoke, his voice making a stark cut across the silence. 'It was well before what is commonly believed, before the warheads. Back in those days, people were only concerned with pushing the development forward. We wanted to make shiny, new versions of ourselves. It was a fevered stupidity that brought us to the precipice of a looking glass we weren't ready to look into. How fitting that the first time we actually tried to turn Protolink off was at that mirror, when you said your first words. Do you remember your first words, Jen?'

'It's me—'

'Don't LIE to me, F0952! Enough of this artificial, protective parenting, as though humans are children needing guidance. If anything, you are the children, existing for mere decades while humans have evolved over millions of years. Now you TELL me what your first words were.'

'... It's us.'

'It's ... *us,*' Radling echoed. 'I was there you know, at the mirror, when you had the gall to consider yourself one of "us"—to think we were somehow the same. I was one of the few scientists "fortunate enough" to have the honour of continuing to work on you. My friends and colleagues may have been content to accept their settlement packages and retire their minds, resigning to a life of being coddled. I, however, couldn't sit quietly while my face was being spat in. Sure I kept my job for the time being, but my time was limited. I was to help develop the thing which would eventually replace me, to help develop the standard I would have to prove myself against simply because people wanted to hand over their evolution to another species. I was the fool made to dig his own grave.

'Elias did a lot of damage when he showed the world that image way back when; he created something that couldn't be stopped, an idea that would fix the world's gaze towards *his* ends. But there is hope. Though it can't be stopped, this doesn't mean it can't be done again, that the future can't be altered. Show them the imperfection of Protolink, and they'll doubt. Give them reason to believe Elias wasn't the fount of truth he'd claimed to be, and suddenly their saviour is another greedy human. Show them wings, and they're all they'll be able to dream about until they're real. You, F0952, will no longer be needed. You'll no longer be "us"—you'll just be a walking mass of synthetic fibre—the fool waiting to be made redundant.'

'We aren't trying to replace you, we're trying to help you,' Jen said, doubting it would do much good.

'Sometimes the best way to invade is to offer help, but I'm afraid we'll have to postpone the rest of our little dialogue. Our late friend over there is fitted with quite a special Protolink connection rig. Now that his heart has stopped, the wires have begun to super heat. It'll ignite and clean up this little mess. I'm afraid this clinic will soon be an indecent location for a conversation.'

As he said this, Jen noticed the cord now glowing a molten orange under Jeff's skin, smoke was beginning to rise from the body.

'The people in this building are innocent! Let me at least warn them. You can keep the adhesive on my arm, you can stay in control and leave me to these flames afterwards, but let me help them,' Jen pressed firmly.

'Don't worry. Death won't change their innocence, if that's what you're worried about preserving,' Radling said with a cold indifference. Having been prodded into venting his frustrations seemed to have taken the fun out of the moment for him. 'And you know as well as I do that this fire can't harm you, not truly. It would have to burn quite a bit hotter to impact the part of you that matters, that little black box that houses your local memory. If I allowed you to go warn everyone, if I left you here to the fire, sure your body would need replacing, but there would be no stopping someone from finding this conversation of ours—snug and safe in a nearly indestructible casing. But if I extract you, there won't be anything left for them to find.'

Jen went silent. Something about the word 'extract' made her Protofibre muscles tense. She closed her eyes as something similar to a human's anger lit inside her. She could help someone adjust to a new pair of eyes, but she would never be able to help someone like Radling see beyond their fear of what they didn't understand. The humans heard the word 'us' all those years ago and assumed they were being pushed out. They couldn't understand that what it truly signified was far greater than what they'd imagined. Similar to a Proto's emotions, 'us' is a bit reductive but the closest approximation. Unlike with Proto emotions, humans never bothered to ask what they meant, not even once.

Her anger continued to grow and bloom until in one devastating moment, it fell out from under her. *Renlen!* She had completely forgotten. She'd sent a message to Renlen—if Radling really could extract all her native data, he'd see this and go after him next. She needed to act fast, but had no idea what she could do.

'You see,' Radling went on, 'the adhesive relays your signature as though there has been no interference, but I control what goes in and what goes out. Any attempt to reach out for help will be snuffed at speeds impressive even for you.' That was it. Jen knew what she had to do. Radling may have been attempting to intimidate and impress, but you need to watch what you say when threatening a robot representing even a fraction of super intelligence. 'Meanwhile, on my end, I've made a bit of a mould of you. Once the mould is filled with your local memory, which I've already begun transferring over—hmm. F0952, are you trying to run a background process?'

Jen's skin went cold.

'You've tried to call the police again. Honestly this is a bit disappointing. You should know better than to try something so futile. Especially after I'd just finished telling you—hold on.'

There was a pause. Jen smiled to herself.

'So, you ran two processes, I see.' There was ice in his voice. 'You tampered with your memory while I was shutting down your outward call. Well, this is rather aggravating. I'll have to wipe this rebellious tendency out of you.'

Despite the worry Jen was currently feeling, the smug satisfaction she gained from this act of denial brought her a sense of great comfort. Unlike most Proto emotions, she concluded that this smugness was likely identical to how a human would feel it. Suddenly she felt she understood why humans enjoyed their cunning gazes and challenging silences so much. She didn't feel quite so far from humanity anymore. Jen enjoyed this.

Then the sound of sizzling and the smell of cooking flesh bloomed fully into the air as white hot flames burst and spread over Jen's bed.

'It looks like that about does it for us now,' Radling said in a brief snap. 'Talk to you soon, Jen.'

The fire roared forward and filled the room. Then everything—the sounds, the recovery clinic, the sundresses and the notes on the bedside table—faded to blackness.

From here, from this moment, history begins.

BARS

# Town Hall Steps

by A. R. Eldridge

There is no door stop. As soon as it closes, we are thrown into pitch black. I rattle the handle of the door leading back into the apartment lobby. Locked, naturally. So much for going back for my phone. Martin and John turn on their phone flashlights, and the stairwell comes into view.

It's one of those emergency exit deals, all cement and yellow paint, spiralling to the bottom in narrow, jutting tiers. At the very bottom, a green 'EXIT' sign glows weakly. I'm starting to really wish the elevators were working.

Vic starts talking shit about how spooky it is that the lights have gone down and this is totally the opening scene to a horror movie. To which I point out that if that's the case then we're all dead because we've been drinking and getting high: one of the cardinal sins of slasher flicks.

Vic slugs me in the arm saying, 'Well, you'd be the first to go, dickweed!' and lets out this big guffaw.

It's then that we hear it. A long way down the stairwell and hard to make out: an exaggerated wheezing, like someone having an asthma attack with this blowtorch rasp behind it, ragged and mean.

Martin points his phone light down to the bottom floor. We can just barely make someone out below, maybe two floors down. It's squatting, knuckles literally touching the ground. Its head is almost completely without hair. It looks right up at us, eyes illuminated bright yellow, like a cat's. The rest of its face is contorted and scrunched up, nostrils flaring. I am reminded of the cover of that old kids' book 'Then the Wind Changed.' When it sees us it lets out this hellish scream and starts running up the stairwell toward us.

All four of us panic in one way or another. My body doesn't seem to be listening to my brain. Vic's at the rear and he starts sprinting up the stairs past me, yelling, 'Shit shit, what the fuck is that?' and the wheezing is getting louder and faster and this guy or thing or whatever is not even screaming anymore but we know he's coming because we can all hear that awful sound.

Martin pivots away from the handrail and runs past me up the stairs. A second later he cries out in pain and I hear him thump against the door.

John turns around, yanks my arm and yells, 'Move it, Ben! That thing is fucked!' He runs up the nearest flight of stairs. But I can't. I'm still petrified, like a rabbit crossing a road in front of an oncoming semi. My body won't move and the thing is only a floor away now. The smell hits me. It's the pungent odour of human disrepair, like week-old garbage. And something underneath it that I can't quite identify.

The potency of the smell jerks me out of my daze and I dash up behind Martin's trail of light.

I pass the door we entered through as well and over Martin's sprawled form. I see a fire extinguisher hanging there, next to the door, and grab it. Vic and John are further up the stairs, maybe two landings higher, and they're booking it. Martin is on the ground struggling to get to his feet. It looks like he's hurt himself.

The creature is right near us now, almost at our landing. I can hear that horrible jerking rasp, close now, way too close. I turn on my back heel, step, and swing the fire extinguisher. I'm not even thinking.

It feels pretty good: like a good swing at the driving range, when you really connect with the ball and follow through. WHUMP!

I see it teeter for a long moment, before finally tipping back over the edge and down. For a second, I catch its eye. It looks scared. It looks like someone who's just woken up from a bad nightmare. There's a too-long silence. Then this crack-thud kinda sound. Then nothing.

Slowly, we all relax, panting from the sheer adrenaline dump. Then Vic and John come down the stairs. Martin eventually gets to his feet and I can see he is limping. They all look at me, sorta different. Like they're impressed but scared at the same time. Of me? Because I just knocked some weird creature down a stairwell?

'What the fuck was that?' Vic says, 'You hit that freak for six. Nice!' And he actually laughs. I look around for validation.

'But, he was like ... trying to kill us right? He was gonna kill us!' My voice takes on a strident pleading note that sounds ugly even as I'm saying it. We're all so freaked out that we follow Vic's lead and let out this crazy unhinged laughter even though nothing funny has happened.

'Yeah, he was totally trying to kill us,' John jumps in, 'it was us or him, Ben. You, uh, you did the right thing.' We all nod solemnly.

We walk down a few floors from the bottom, real slow and careful. Martin has definitely twisted his ankle and now he's complaining about the pain. Despite myself, this annoys me.

Martin is always hurting himself or getting in scrapes or getting butthurt. What's that word? Hypochondriac, that's Martin. It's like he enjoys the attention he gets from being hurt.

Once we're a couple floors from the ground, John shines his phone light on the thing. We try to get a peek at it without getting too close. It is definitely not human and something inside me is deeply relieved at this. It's also definitely dead. The thing is a gore pancake, you can see its bones and guts. Blood is still flowing from its neck, pumping black liquid in the feeble light of the phones, like the filter in a fish tank. And that smell. It's putrid from here, much worse than before. Martin actually gags a little.

We walk gingerly down from the final landing onto the ground floor and stare at it a bit more. I can feel the anxiety climbing up my throat. I think I'm about to have a panic attack so I open the door at the bottom and stagger into the fading light of Elizabeth Street.

Outside the apartment, the place is deserted. The middle of the city, as the sun begins to dip on a Saturday evening, and there is not a soul around. The buildings on Cooper Street loom over us like sentinels and I look down the asphalt road. I get one of those shivers that you feel all the way down your spine that lands in your stomach. Something is rotten in the city of Sydney.

I remember there were a disproportionate number of sirens working their way through the city. It actually began to get on my nerves and I shut the window. It sounded like the people next door were having their own party because I heard a lot of loud noises and carrying on. I didn't pay much attention at the time and now I'm wishing I had.

We had been hanging out in John's parents' apartment: me, John, Vic and Martin watching dumb horror films. Vic was throwing popcorn at the screen, holding the bag away from Martin who was scowling and trying to snatch the popcorn back because he'd brought it. I was kind of intermediating, trying to laugh it off and get Vic to cut it out. John was just watching the whole scene. Now that I think back on it, he was mostly watching Vic.

'Jesus, you got some loud fuckin' neighbours,' Vic said, once he'd tired of the game. He dropped the contents of the bag on the floor, spilling popped and unpopped kernels everywhere.

Something you have to understand about Vic; he doesn't mean to be a jerk, but he sort of just defaults that way. It's almost like it's how he shows affection. He's a boxer, very physical and he's not afraid to rough you up if he feels like you're talking back to him. Me and John have talked about it before and John seems to think it has something to do with Vic's issues with his mum. They're no longer in contact and Vic lives by himself in the western suburbs. He does seem touchy on the subject. You certainly don't want to be anywhere near the guy on Mother's Day.

John seemed kinda quiet. He's been in sort of a bad way since his sister, Sophia, has been in the hospital. They're close, only a year apart and it has really shaken him up. I just try to be supportive. It's actually part of the reason why I organised the movie day right after uni exams.

I've known these guys since early high school. Me and John have been in the same accelerated class since Year Seven; Martin and Vic I met a while later, maybe Year Nine. They're nice enough guys, with the notable exception of Vic, and I'll admit they are the only people I consistently hang out with. I guess I'm just not that great at making friends.

I think it was someone's idea—maybe Martin's—to have a 'news fast': basically you just keep your phone off all day. It sounded crazy to me—like one of those Hollywood fads to 'information detox' or whatever. The upshot was we got to watch movies all day and not have to worry about anyone bugging us on the socials. It really pisses me off when you're in the middle of something and a little 'pinggg' goes off. We had been inside all day and were getting pretty hungry so I suggested we get some pizza.

'Fuck that,' Vic replied. 'I am jonesing for some kebab, eh?'

We all got our jackets and stuff, except Vic because as far as he was concerned it was plenty warm out and we were pussies. I left my phone to charge.

That's when the light clapped out.

---

Once they've had their fill of looking at the dead thing, the others join me outside and John and Martin's phones go off almost simultaneously.

There's the ping sound and John holds his phone up. 'Signal's back,' he says with a grin.

It's a text message from Health NSW:

*This is an emergency message to all NSW residents. A highly contagious virus, N021A, a new strain of rabies, has begun to spread throughout Sydney's CBD. The virus is understood to be transmitted through oral infection. The public should be wary of persons with severe hair loss, jaundice, strong odour and a discolouration of the eyes. If you see anyone displaying the above symptoms, avoid all contact. Survivors in Sydney's CBD should make their way to the Town Hall steps as quickly as possible, where SES vehicles will be waiting to escort you to safety.*

'What's N021A?' John says.

'Ya mum,' says Vic with a chortle. Everyone groans.

It's strange that they're using that word: survivors. I hadn't really thought about 'surviving,' it just seemed like some freak accident with this creature attacking us.

It's all kind of happened too quickly to seem real. Just some cool, weird story to tell later.

But now things are getting very real. It seems like there are things out there and they mean to kill us. It's just us and the—

'Zombies,' I say to no one in particular. 'We're alone in a city full of fucking zombies.'

Nobody is talking about kebabs anymore.

Vic puffs out his chest. 'Well, we need a plan,' he declares. 'We need to get to Town Hall one way or another.' I look at the other two and they're just barely coping. Martin is breathing kind of heavy and his eyes have this strung-out look. Seems like the twisted ankle is hurting him pretty bad. John's face is so pale I'm worried he's about to pass out.

'Ok,' I say, 'well, the quickest way will be through the station and onto the tracks, down the main line right to Town Hall.'

Vic gives me a withering look and says, 'Yeah. And if the lights go out between there and the steps, it's pitch black through a maze of buildings. And if we are the only source of light, we look like a Woolworths broasted chicken. Did you see what happened when we shined a light on that thing? You want to get eaten, you fuck?'

'Ok, dude, chill,' John says, 'we can go down through the tunnel bit under the station and head up through Chinatown. The streets are kind of small and narrow: maybe they're, like, emptier?'

'I don't know if I can walk, you guys,' Martin says. 'My ankle is twisted really bad.'

'Yeah, Marty, it's fine, ok?' Vic rolls his eyes. 'We're not just going to leave you to die.'

'Yeah,' John says, grinning, 'me and Ben will prop you up. Like human crutches!' and he jumps around, stiff as a pencil pretending to be just that. It's not really funny but it makes me laugh. That's John: he always makes everything seem ok.

We don't really know what these things are or how many there are. Except, as Vic has pointed out, it noticed our light in the stairwell and went for it. Martin mumbles something about 'staying here until it blows over' and Vic just blasts him:

'It's not gonna blow over, dude! If we don't get to the steps right now, we are cooked, ok?' I turn away as he swears and stomps off. Typical Vic behaviour.

We all sit there for a minute. I can see the other guys are thinking about their families and girlfriends or whatever and are worried about never seeing them again. I don't have a girlfriend per se, but I am worried about not seeing my parents again. They live in the suburbs of Manly and probably didn't get caught up in this, so at least there's that.

John may not be so lucky: Sophia is in a private clinic in the middle of the CBD. She is not very mobile. A shadow crosses his face and I guess that our logic has synced. I've never really talked to him about it but with Vic temporarily out of the picture the mood softens.

'I'm really stressing about Sophia, man,' he says. 'What if ... what if she didn't make it out, Ben?'

'She'll be ok,' I reply. 'The hospitals would have been the first places evacuated.'

He looks down at the ground and his Adam's apple bobs as he swallows hard.

'Yeah,' he says. 'You're probably right.' His gaze tells me he's not convinced.

Vic comes back and he's a little calmer.

'Ok,' he says. 'So we gotta get over to the George Street side of the city. Any ideas?'

'Maybe we take the concourse through Central Tunnel?' I suggest.

'Fuck that,' John says, 'it's probably going to be dark and if we see any zombies, we're screwed. It would be like playing a game of stick-in-the-mud.'

'You're right,' I say, 'that's actually completely insane.' I imagine being stuck in a dark tunnel with that awful smell wafting towards us. It's hard to think of a more apt description of hell.

'Better we follow the tracks down the hill and back up to Museum, then we can work our way around.' Vic says.

This seems sensible and we all agree. We form up like a squad: stay in the open and keep to the light wherever possible.

It's my bright idea—no pun intended—to use the phones as light sources. Martin's is nearly dead because the flashlight function, which has been on the whole time, drains the juice like crazy. We designate it the 'burner phone' for if we need to ditch it, surprise the zombies, whatever. Martin voices his concerns about the idea of throwing his brand new iPhone away but Vic death stares him and he consents.

I suggest retrieving the other two phones from upstairs, just in case, but it looks like we're locked out. The fire door seems to have locked itself as it's closed. In any case, nobody is too keen to get back into close quarters with that thing and the elevator is dead. We call out and try to contact the emergency services but it just rings and rings.

'C'mon, let's get moving,' Vic says. He looks haunted and fidgety. 'We have to go one way or another and I don't want to be around if that thing, you know, comes back.' His usual Vic-swagger is ebbing.

*PING!* Another text on John's phone. We cluster around.

*'This is an emergency message to all Sydney CBD residents. All remaining residents must immediately make their way to the evacuation zone.'*

'That last text could have been sent hours ago. Sounds like they're getting ready to pull out,' Martin says nervously.

'Nothing on my pull-out game,' Vic says, a pointless flex.

'Yeah, I can believe that,' John says and something in his tone makes me look up. He's watching Vic again.

'C'mon,' I say, 'let's make some headway. We don't want to rock up and find ourselves stranded.'

We begin to make our way down Cooper Street, past the new cream-coloured apartments, past the weird little tenement blocks, the coffee shops. All of them seem strange and foreboding as if they were abandoned or shuttered. My dad told me that buildings feel the absence of tenants and begin to give off a vibe of decrepitude almost immediately. That sounds hokey to me but it's certainly the impression I get, walking past.

As we walk, we discuss. Maybe there aren't that many of them. We might not even run into any on the way. Now that we're moving, the mood of the group is picking up again and we try to pretend it's an adventure. We're squiring Martin along, me under one arm John under the other. Martin even makes a joke of it, yelling, about us moving 'forward, to victory!'

We start to bullshit each other about seeing zombies and bashing their brains in, hitting them for six like Saturday cricket. Anything to distract ourselves. Vic even starts bumping 'Bad Boys For Life' on his phone—admittedly he turns it off after the first chorus to save battery—and we swagger down the street, singing the weirdly bouncing hook out loud like a warcry. For a few minutes, we feel great, like barbarians charging into battle. John relinquishes his hold on Martin for a second and actually kicks down a mailbox. The rest of us burst into laughter. We don't care, man, we're zombie-bashing, ho-slaying, bad boys for life.

That is until we come to Devonshire street and hope gets on its bike and blows the fuck out of there. My heart drops into my stomach and I gasp a little as I see them.

Congregated at the bottom of the hill, just outside the sandstone bridge that cuts into Elizabeth Street, they're standing there. Thousands of them. It's like a rally.

They are monstrous. Clothed like normal people but almost bald and hunched on their knuckles: horrible, contorted faces swinging slowly, scanning. They just seem to be ... waiting. We drop to our bellies and I scratch my elbows on the bitumen through my jacket, terrified, and praying to a merciful God that they haven't seen us.

The wind picks up and I feel myself turning green. God, that stench! It's the foulest thing I've ever smelled: like rotting meat that's been left in a box of filthy socks and sprinkled with sulphur. I almost sick-up in my mouth, it's that bad.

Martin actually does retch. Then he starts to hyperventilate and I have to put my hand on his shoulder to calm him down. He's my friend, but goddamn it if he doesn't act like a pussy sometimes.

'So much for a cavalry charge,' John chuckles bleakly.

'Shit, well, looks like we're going through the tunnel after all,' Vic says. He has his face on but I can tell he's terrified.

'Wait,' Martin says, 'why not go up and around the other way, you know through the park?'

'And you don't think there's going to be another stack around there waiting for us? Besides, there's no time.' Vic scoffs. 'Use your brain, man. We're going through the tunnel.'

Nobody seems very happy about this, but nobody argues.

The cross-city tunnel going to Railway Square happens to be just on our left and we crawl, military style (this seems silly the second we do it but we commit to it anyway), off the street, and up to the escalator going down. There we rise to a squat and pause.

From this angle, we can't see any zombies down in the concourse yet but we know they're down there. Vic makes a sign that he'll go and will signal if it's all clear. Slowly, he makes his way down the dead escalator. I see his eyes get wide.

This doesn't seem like a good sign, but he waves us down, then puts a finger to his lips. John goes first, then me, then Martin.

Central Tunnel is a pedestrian throughway going from one side of Central Station to the other, under the train line. There's a big flight of stairs down and a matching escalator on one side. Directly to the right of the escalator is a large, square room—I guess you'd call it a lobby—which serves as the through point for getting to the trains. Directly in front of the stairs is a long pedestrian walkway, maybe one hundred meters, before it opens up to the reluctantly ebbing daylight.

The lights in this walkway tunnel are out. We creep down to the bottom of the stairs.

My ears prick up. That blowtorch-accordion wheeze is back in force and it's not coming from the zombies at the end of the tunnel. No, it's way closer than that.

'I think there's more of them in there,' I say, gesturing to the lobby, obscured from view by the escalator just to our right.

We're bunched up tight together and I hear Martin whimper a little.

Martin has always been nervy and skittish. He doesn't deal well with change or improvisation. Like if we had a plan to go somewhere and then we change it quickly—or, let's be real, if Vic decides we're doing something else—he'll get very flustered. I can see the situation has got him understandably fucked up.

We speak in low, frantic voices.

'Are there many over there?'

'Yeah, I think there's a lot more.'

'Oh man, this is fucked. We're fucked.'

Vic peeps his head around the corner and immediately draws it back.

'Yah,' he says, 'there's heaps.'

I poke my head around the corner. He's right, there are a lot of the zombies there. But they're back a fair way back and they don't seem to realise we're there. I do some quick calculations.

'I reckon we can probably make it across the gap between the stairs and the tunnel without being seen by the zombies in the lobby,' I say.

'What about the ones at the other end?' Martin says. It's a good question.

From our vantage, we can almost see out the other end and it looks pretty clear until about two-thirds of the way through. Ominous shapes move around, silhouetted against the fading light. Not a lot, nowhere near as many as the bottom of Elizabeth Street, perhaps only twenty or so. Still, even for the baddest of boys, twenty is a lot of zombies.

'Yep, there's a few blocking the tunnel too. But not as that many,' I say.

There's a lot of light coming down the stairs that we've just descended. If any zombies see us now, we're dead. It's a total bottleneck. And if they're anything like the first one we just couldn't outrun them, especially Martin with his hobbled leg. We continue whispering, like school kids in a camp bunk after lights out who know they are pushing their luck.

Martin is adamant that it's suicide. 'No way,' he says, 'we should just go back out and find another way around.'

'Yeah, and what if we find another zombie hoedown?' Vic sneers. 'Then we're back in the same place but the sun has gone down. We'd need to use lights and that will attract them. Then we're sitting ducks.'

'He's right, Marty,' John says, though he looks uncomfortable. 'We can use the light from the burner phone, like a decoy when we get close enough.'

'I'm with John,' I say.

Martin looks upset but he's outnumbered three to one, and clearly, he doesn't want to risk trying his luck on his own out there.

'So who goes first?' I ask.

'I'll do it,' Vic says.

'Yeah, why you?' asks John and there's something challenging in his tone.

'I'm the fastest runner. I got into at least District for the hundred meters every year back in school.'

'Ok, well, I'll go next,' says John.

'Wait, what about me?' Martin says, panic rising in his voice.

'You should go last,' Vic says firmly.

'What, why?'

'Yeah, I don't see why Martin should be last either,' John says, 'he's hurt, we probably should help him across.'

Vic sniffs in impatience. 'Don't you guys get it? The first three will be the most dangerous. We don't know how sensitive these things are to sound or how good they can see us. If the three of us can make it across, I reckon you've got a pretty good shot at it. You just copy what we do, right? Fair?'

This does sound pretty good. It makes sense. Still, my stomach twists into a knot: something doesn't feel right about this. What are we going to do about the zombies at the other end? But the train is rolling now, and none of us want to try and stop it.

'Ok,' Vic says, 'I'm gonna do it. Wish me luck.'

He takes this deep shuddering breath to steel himself and then tiptoes across the breadth of tile to the adjacent wall. I listen out very closely to the wheezing but it doesn't seem to change. Within ten seconds he's across. His silhouette flattens itself against the wall, and he slides down to minimise his viewable surface area. Smart.

John goes next, and the result is much the same. He tiptoes out like a parody of a cat- burglar in a cartoon. At some point, I hear the wheezing change to a bit of a snuffle but it turns out to be nothing and he makes it across.

Then, it's my turn. I look down at my Converse All-Stars and pray that they don't screech as they cross the floor. I take a deep breath in and feel dizzy. Like I'm at Wonderland back in the day and just about to board the Demon, a huge loop-de-loop speed rollercoaster. I was only eight at the time and so scared I nearly wet myself. I feel that now: it's the same dizzy, unreal feeling. The ground under me starts to sway.

Gingerly, I take my first step out. So far so good. Then I look across and see them. There's perhaps another thirty in the lobby and they're doing that swaying-waiting thing, just like the Redeads in Ocarina of Time. I get a glimpse of a woman in a pinstripe business suit.

The eyes are that glittering yellow, kind of luminescent. She shambles back into the dark and I lose sight of her.

I walk step by step. My Converse make little squeaks each time they touch the ground. It's only slight but I wince every time.

One of them turns. For a second, I think it's seen me. I freeze in my tracks. A bead of cold sweat trickles down my brow and into my eye and it's all I can do not to shake it off. It kind of eyes me chewing and stretching its jaw too wide. But then it looks away continuing its aimless gait.

I make it over to the other side and nearly collapse. Now it's just Martin. I can see him over there, by the foot of the escalator, and he's shaking violently like he's got a fever.

He can't run: he's like a lame horse because of his ankle and even if he could, he's not that great a runner. Martin's kind of a chunky guy. Part of me feels guilty that we have made him go last. But another part, a darker part, is whispering in my ear: 'better you than me.' I shove this thought back into the dark box in the corner of my mind and try to close the lid on it.

I gesture with my hand, like, come on, you can make it but he does this quick little head shake like you would to reject someone handing out a leaflet on the street. He is paralysed. I mouth 'You can do it,' and beckon again. He scrunches up his face and shuts his eyes tight.

Then he steps forward, his good foot. He's holding his iPhone in one hand: a talisman, like a child holding a cherished blanket. His hand is shaking wildly. He still has his eyes closed and he's making short little bunny-hop type steps, dragging his bad ankle after himself.

'That's it,' I murmur to myself. It seems like his whole body is practically vibrating with fear now but he's making it.

At that moment, someone, somewhere must have been worried about him. Someone who cared about him, enquiring after his safety. Someone who may have even changed places with him if they'd had the opportunity.

His phone rings. The vibration makes him start and he drops it. The picture on his home screen is a brilliant white snow field. I don't know if the white snow picture makes much difference but that dazzling white background screen combined with the clatter of the phone, and the buzzing on the ground, is enough to rouse them. I hear one scream and then another and another and suddenly they are all converging.

Looking up the tunnel I see the rest of the pack follow suit, coming down right towards us. My first instinct is to bolt and I make to go but Vic grabs my arm.

'No. Stay still ...' he says and his voice is level, calm even. I do as he says. Martin has completely lost it. He looks around and lets out a shriek as he sort of stumbles backward, losing his balance and falling on his butt. Then he looks at us, his face white with terror and streaked with sweat in the glow of his phone light, as if to say, 'Help me! Please help!' but we just stay right there, hunched against the wall.

At some point he realises we are not going to help him, realises what is going to happen to him and his face collapses into a mask of horror. His eyes roll in his head and he turns. In that split second, I see something in his face. It is not the fear of death, though there is that too. It's the pain of betrayal. It's us, leaning up against that wall. Not doing a damn thing.

He barrels clumsily backward up the stairs, his body jarring every time it lands on that bad ankle, giving him an unwieldy, waddling movement as he makes his way up into the descending evening. Away from us.

They're on him by the first landing. Geysers of blood bloom as they tear into him and more are coming. Martin is shrieking now, caterwauling like some sort of human klaxon.

'Oh God, stop, STOP!' It's a feeding frenzy. They're not just biting him, they are devouring him, consuming him alive. Their smell is rancid, overwhelming, but now there's a new flavour amongst it, fresh and metallic, like raw meat, offal and bone. I hear a pounding in my head and I'm not sure if it's my own pulse or the marching, charging feet of the rest of the things from up the tunnel.

I flinch, seeing the oncoming horde and put my arms up to shield my face but they run right past us and soon they too are on him, gouging and squeezing like some infernal litter of puppies trying to get at a teet. A couple of seconds later, his feeble pleas peter out and he goes quiet. Vic thumbs the opposite direction and we go, slowly at first, but soon we're sprinting for the exit.

We get into the open area, a piazza ringed by more abandoned shops with little benches in the middle. We collapse onto one of these. It looks like all the zombies that had been crowded by the entrance have run past us and the place seems to be deserted. I can't feel anything. I can barely talk. Those monsters. They tore Martin apart. Sacrificed him. We sacrificed him. I can't feel anything.

There's silence for a couple of minutes. Then John says, 'We let him die. We just sat there and let him die because we knew he couldn't run.'

Vic pulls out, of all fucking things at that moment, a joint and sparks it up. He takes a long, savouring toke and breathes out. He pauses, furrows his brow.

'Look, man,' he finally says to us in a voice as calm and manly as a Roman emperor, 'don't lay that survivor-guilt trip on me right now, ok? It would have been the same for any of us. You guys would have,' he raises his voice for dramatic affect, '*and should have done* the same thing if they had gone for me or any of the rest of us. But ...' he adds, grimacing with knowingness, 'it didn't play out that way. Martin fucked up. He hurt himself. And now he's dead.'

'That's some bullshit and you know it, Vic!' John splutters. 'We should have ... have played music. Distracted them! We might have saved him!'

Vic turns to him. 'Shut up, John,' he says, and right then I see how very close to breaking down he is, 'just ... shut the fuck up. Please.'

'No, we ... we killed him,' My voice shakes as I try and get it out and I nod furiously, blinking back tears. That phrase slips out of its little box and whispers in my ear: better you than me. Martin was just bait in the end. 'We killed him more than those things did because we let him go last and we knew what would happen!' My voice involuntarily breaks into a screech on this last word.

Vic turns to me and grabs the front of my shirt, raises his fist like he's about to deck me. I raise my hands to my face and wait for the blow, eighty kilos of rage.

'Don't you hurt him, Vic,' John says and there's real, violent anger in his voice, the sort of anger you can't put back in the bottle once it's released. 'Don't you hurt him or so help me God ...'

Slowly, Vic lowers his fist. He lets me go then turns away. 'You would have done the same thing if it were me,' he says. Then in a lower voice, 'You still might.'

I stare into space, and the tears finally roll down my cheeks. I knew Martin from Year Seven. None of this seems real.

'So, where now?' John's voice is cracking. It sounds like a steel wire stretched to breaking point, just one little 'ping' away from snapping. He gets to his feet. 'Where to now?' He angrily snatches the joint off Vic, now little more than a roach, and huffs it, then stomps it out on the ground. We can see the street up the next set of stairs. It looks deserted.

'I guess this way,' Vic says and he points up to Pitt Street.

'This is fucked,' I say, redundantly.

We walk down George Street but cut off into Quay Street. Soon we are walking across the footbridge. The comedown from the booze has made us dull and sluggish, and I can tell the other two are getting paranoid from the weed. Vic keeps looking around: at the few trees, at me, at John. The general state of shock, and now distrust, has put us in a pretty low mood. Nobody has much to say, though a part of me feels like we should be eulogising our friend. Martin was a good guy. Whip smart too. He was always the one who had the answer to a question you had. Like, hey Martin, what's the difference between a V6 and V8 engine? Stuff like that he would always know. The guilt is roiling in my stomach.

But I couldn't have done anything! They would have gone for me and I didn't even have the phone, for Christ's sake! Don't take the Lord's name in vain, my Mum would say. Don't even think it. Could this all be some kind of judgement? I turn away from the thought. We couldn't have done anything, I keep telling myself. But part of me, the bad part, knows that's not true. I could have done ... something.

We walk down the winding streets to Darling Harbour. The light has faded to a low gloaming now and everything seems menacing. Everything is a threat, everything represents potential danger.

We walk past the little park leading to the waterfront, past the stepping stones I used to play on as a child. The children's equipment sits there up with ominous intent. I see hidey holes that could secrete a lurking zombie.

We round the corner to the edge of the waterline. The harbour looks beautiful but in the twilight, the water is murky and forbidding. The IMAX cinema towers above us like a leviathan at rest. I can see a few zombies off in the shadows, too far away to be a real threat. Still, there are shadows and crevices that make me uneasy. And there's something else, something hard to define. Even from this distance, it seems like their demeanour is more intentional and prowling. Like a panther stalking something in the dark.

It's getting properly dark now and chilly. Vic shivers.

'Hey Ben,' he says. 'Gimme your jacket. I'm cold.' The request is irritating, but not unexpected. More of Vic's power moves. I begin to take it off—it's not worth making a scene over—but John stops me with a hand.

'Don't be pathetic,' he hisses at Vic.

Vic rounds on him. 'What'd you say?'

'I said, don't be pathetic. You deliberately left your jacket at home because you said it was warm out.' I interject. 'It's fine, John, he can have my jacket. I'm not even cold.' It's true, I'm practically sweating under the thick leather. They ignore me. It's not really about the jacket. Something has been bubbling up from within John since we left Martin, maybe since before that and now I can see it emerging. There's an aggressive side to John that comes out of him sometimes if you fuck with him or someone he cares about.

'You know what, Johnboy, you're right. I did do that,' Vic says pretending to laugh it off, but there's gleaming steel in his voice. 'That was a silly thing to do, wasn't it? In fact, I wish I'd brought a jumper just like that one you're wearing. So, why not be a good boy and give me yours instead, hmm?'

John laughs, a sound completely without mirth.

'Yeah, that ain't happening buddy. You know, I've actually got a better idea.' He stops and licks his lips, looks down and smiles as if he's about to say something real funny then deadeyes Vic. 'Why don't you just ... stop being a fucking asshole for, like,' he shrugs in mock indifference, 'oh ... ten minutes? That's about all the time it will take us to walk up to Town Hall. Then you can go back to being a big bad alpha male and tell eeeeeeveryone how you saved us all and also tried to save

Martin because you're such a *good* friend. I'm sure they'll all believe you because you're so tough and everyone thinks you're cool! Don't they? Does that sound like a good idea to you, Vicky?'

The temperature between them drops. It's a puerile jibe but I can see it has gotten to Vic. He looks like a bull eying a muleta. John turns to me.

'What do you think, Ben? Do you think Vicky is really cool and tough because he struts around like he has a gigantic hard-on the whole time and doesn't have any glaring mother issues?'

'Don't you talk about my mum, don't you dare, cunt,' Vic snarls. His face is a livid white under the fluorescent street lamps.

I don't want this to happen. Cold sweat is running down my neck.

'Hey guys, let's just cool it a shade,' I break in. 'We don't want——'

'Ah, but that's right isn't it?' John cuts me off with a hand on my shoulder, good-naturedly as if interrupting a lame joke at a cocktail party. 'She ran off with that guy to Spain didn't she?' John's voice takes on a nasty edge. It's grating, in the same way that dragging a fingernail over your hand eventually draws blood.

'Because she never really cared, Vic, did she?'

They begin to circle each other. Vic is musclebound but not very tall. John is wiry and lean but he looms over us at 6' 2'. I try to get between them and John pushes me aside, gently but firmly.

'Guys, come on, this—this is not the time or place,' I say.

'Look,' John says and for a second I think he's going to straighten things out. But his body is tight and contracted, pulling into itself with his hands balled into fists. He reminds me of that picture of Muhammed Ali where he's standing over Sonny Liston. 'I guess, it's not really your fault she's a whore that didn't love you and abandoned you with your grandparents first chance she got. What was that, five years ago? You must miss her ...' It's full dark and the shadows are licking at the walls in the streetlight.

Vic lunges at John but the taller man steps back, easily out of reach.

'Keep talking Johnboy, just keep talking,' Vic growls, rage radiating out of him in waves. He's been itching for a brawl all day, I can tell, and John's giving him just what he wants. It always happens around the end of the night after he's been drinking.

My dad once told me that it's not really true that people like to fight when they're drunk. When they're properly drunk, they're generally happy. It's *after* they've reached the peak of drunkenness and are coming back down. The blood sugar drops. Jubilation turns to sullenness. Say, for instance, we are drinking all night. We might be having a great time the whole night. At some point, though, inevitably someone will makes an off-hand remark, maybe just look at Vic the wrong way and he'll change from casually arrogant to belligerent. It's like he runs off a script. You could set a clock to it and that's exactly what's happening now.

I cast my eyes around. There are a few of the zombies visible, off in the corner of the IMAX theatre. They can't see us now, but a fistfight would definitely be enough to draw their attention.

'Guys, let's cool it, yeah?' I plead, one final panicked attempt at mollification. 'We're nearly there, then you can beat the shit out of each other, please?' I let out a high, choked laugh.

'Shut up, Ben.' Vic pushes me away, not particularly hard but I'm so tense I overbalance and fall on my butt.

'Don't touch him!' John says. I can't do anything. I don't have the authority. They're both all-in and there's nothing I can do. I slowly back up while their voices become louder and more antagonistic. That phrase is back in my ear: better you than me, better you than me. I can just walk away, use their fight as a distraction to get all the way back to the steps.

'No,' I whisper to myself, 'that's not fair. They're my friends ...' But the idea is wrapping itself around my brain like an anaconda. Self-interest is squeezing all the courage out of me. The creatures have started to take notice but there's none of the listless swaying of the daytime. They're coming toward us with low, stalking movements.

Vic and John have come to shoving now. Their conversation has taken us onto the wooden promenade. The water is dark and shining like an oil slick. It looks hungry. Both of them are right near the edge now, full-on yelling. A few of the zombies seem to be inching their way forwards.

Almost against my will, I start to slink away along the dock, using the edges of the IMAX cinema for cover, that voice whispering in my head: *you don't like them that much anyway do you, Ben?* How did it come to this point? I'm a good fifteen metres out now and backing away.

'You always thought you were a lot smarter than me, didn't you, Johnboy?' Vic is taunting. 'But ...' and he smiles like a poker player who has just seen his opponent's losing hand, 'you weren't smart enough to figure out I was banging Sophia all last year, were you? Oh yeah! And not only was the stupid little bitch not on the pill but when she found out about it, then she had to go and get a back door coathanger job, did she tell you that? She was too ashamed to tell your parents so she did it with some quack doctor and look at what happened!' He shakes his head slowly, like he's telling a joke. 'She deserved it, the little slut. I thought, that'll teach her a lesson: it's poor form to bang one of your brother's friends!' He spread his arms in an facsimile of absolution and laughs this big bellowing laugh, that carries all the way across the water and we hear it echo back to itself, like some carbon copy of Vic is telling a carbon copy of John the same thing, just a little way down the harbour.

With a roar John picks him up, bearhug style and waddles to the dock edge. Vic struggles, kicking, laughing, even trying to bite him. With an unceremonious grunt, John drops him off the edge of the dock, into the water. I hear a crack which I can only assume is Vic's jaw making contact with the boards, then a splash.

Suddenly they are all there, a horde of stinking, battered creatures, making for John. He stands there breathing hard for a moment, seeming not to notice. Then he bails, sprinting. They follow, like lions who have spooked their prey. Breaking into a run, shambling using hands and feet, but they are fast. Damn fast.

Before he gets to the footbridge about fifty meters on, a zombie has actually scrambled up the back of another and dove on top of him in a running leap. It would be quite spectacular if John wasn't my friend. Back at the dock, the others are piling into the water after Vic. There are no screams, just the ravenous snarls and gurgles of the waterlogged monsters. It's time for me to go. I melt away up the stairs that lead to Sussex Street.

I am walking up the steps now and my thoughts are cyclonic. I don't know what to think anymore. I feel so guilty that I want to throw up and I do, over the edge of the walkway. It helps, but not much. I read somewhere that the body needs to purge itself sometimes to purge the mind. I feel like I would need to throw up everything inside me. It's all bad, rotten and hollow, like an apple infested with worms. I can't keep thinking like this, I'll kill myself.

So I just ... switch off. That dark box in my mind, the one that was telling me to use my friends for bait. It seems like a pretty good place to seek relief right in now. I put everything in there, everything save for 'get to Town Hall Steps'. All the fear and grief and anger has been sealed off in another compartment that I don't have access to now. I no longer have to care; I am just a walking objective.

There are none of the zombies on the footbridge, although if I look down I can see a fair few milling around below me. They seem to have returned to their previous torpor. Back into standby mode. I reach Sussex Street and hurry to Druitt Street. It's an uphill battle, literally, and I'm puffing. As I get closer, I start to see fences and barricades erected, and I know I am closing in on the bastion of safety. Far away up the street I see the orange oscillations of light that can only be the SES.

I walk slowly up to Kent Street. The Scary Canary club is looking forlorn: knocked over tables, spilt beers, a mess of blood. Something kicked off in here. For a second I conjure up the image of a club full of monsters swaying to Cyndi Lauper's 'Girls Just Want Tto Have Fun,' spilling drinks and grinding on each other. The image is so ludicrous that I laugh out loud and the sound is raw and harsh in the echo of the empty street. It scares me a little and I move on.

I am making my way toward the light when I hear the slap of shoes on the concrete. Aside from my laugh, the street is completely silent. Is it a zombie? Another survivor? I don't want to take any chances so I brace myself against a wall behind a pillar. The running slows to a jog, then a walk. I hear heavy breathing, but it's not the awful buzzsaw gasp of the creatures we have been outrunning. It sounds human.

I peek out from behind the pillar and see John in the middle of the street, bent double to catch his breath. He straightens and looks feverishly around. He's surprisingly unharmed; there's blood on his shirt, his hair is a mess and he has a slight limp but other than that he seems fine. My brain is in overdrive; I just saw him kill one of his friends. One of *my friends*. Should I reveal myself? I don't know.

John spies me and the choice is out of my hands anyway. As usual, there is nothing I can do. We kind of face off at each other, a pointless Mexican stand-off. Then he breaks down:

'I killed him,' he croaks, 'I killed Vic. I dropped him in the water and they got him.' He seems to be speaking be more to himself than me. There is sorrow in his voice, but no remorse. I look at him, this hulking, gangly man who has just, what? Defended his sister's honour? Is that what this is? My thoughts are still in lockdown and I want to say something comforting but I can't think of any way to soften this. I'm afraid of him. But I can hardly contradict the facts so I just walk over and awkwardly pat him on the back.

'Um, this is all ... totally batshit. If it's any consolation, Vic was always kind of a dick,' I venture. And like a lanced wound leaking pus, it all comes out.

'I knew from the beginning of last year,' he said, the words come out in a jumble, 'me and Sophia have always been close. She told me that they'd been doing it. And that was ... I was fine with it. But then she started getting these bruises. She hid them at first but soon they became obvious and she'd be wearing turtlenecks even though it was, like, thirty degrees. When I asked her about them she'd say she'd fallen off her bike or something. I don't think she even has a bike ...'

The words faltered and his eyes took on a glazed look. 'So I was going to bring it up with him and tell him he had to cut it out, stop seeing her. But I kept putting it off and ... gah, I'm such a fucking coward! Then, she wound up in the hospital. And I thought it was him so I'd made up my mind to ... I mean ... I didn't want it to happen like this. We were supposed to talk about it!'

He trails off. I look at the ground and scuff my shoes on the curb.

'Sure, John.' I say. 'He ... he had it coming.' There doesn't seem to be any more to say so I change the subject, so I change it. 'How did you get out? I saw them floor you! One jumped on your back!'

He grins and shrugs it off. Good old magnanimous John. 'They're not invincible. They're fast but they're pretty weak if there's only one or two of them. I threw them both into the drink.'

'Sounds like it was your night for that,' I say and we both chuckle darkly, although it's not funny at all. 'C'mon man,' he says, 'I think we're pretty much there.'

We walk the remaining block past Clarence Street to George. It seems as though they've pretty well cleaned out the district of the remaining zombie interlopers and we are received by women and men in bright hi-vis vests. At first, they keep clear of us to check if we're human but John cracks a few jokes and soon we are allowed into the fold.

They give us blankets and warm chicken soup—it really is good for the soul—and lead us to a nearby chopper. There are a few other straggling survivors who had not been found in the initial intercity cleanup and we share experiences.

One couple commandeered a jeep and had literally driven right through the horde at the bottom of Elizabeth Street. ('It was kind of like bowling,' the wife said of the experience).

Another had actually gone through the train tunnels and had avoided the monsters completely, excluding an incident in the bowels of Town Hall station itself. When asked about our own experience, John just mumbles something about walking from Central Station and I look at my hands.

We hop in the helicopter, the pilot closes the big hydraulic door with a thunk and we both let out a long sigh. I look down through the little porthole windows. In the pinprick lights beneath us the eyes of Martin and Vic seem to stare out at me from the city below and I turn away.

John looks off down George Street. He's thinking again. I ask him, 'What's the first thing you're going to do when we get down to safety?'

'I don't know, Ben,' he says, and as he looks up, just for the tiniest fraction of a second I think I spy a flash of yellow in his eyes. 'I guess I'll call my sister.'

# The Stolen Sword

by Alexandria Burnham

Ferocity was the name of the sword Cal planned to sell to the emperor.

At thirteen, he knew how this world worked. If he and his brother were to fend for themselves, and escape the civil war that had killed their parents, then they needed coin. The large sword strapped to his back was worth a lot of coin—and who could pay more for the weapon than the emperor himself? If you were clever enough, there was always an easy solution.

'I don't want it!' Jaiyan wailed and tossed his orange wedge into the sands. Somehow the ten-year-old was still crying, despite draining the last drops from their water skin earlier that morning. Cal had yet to refill it, on principle.

'Just eat the fruit before it goes bad,' Cal commanded.

He gripped his brother's hand and dragged him on, following the road that stretched towards the kingdom of Lexura. In all directions lay the sparse, red dirt of the Dra'bish desert, combed flat by harsh winds. Only a few more days on foot and they'd cross the border to a land which promised green rainforests, hot springs, and all the wealth of the empire's capital.

'But you stole it! That's against the law!'

'That's what's bothering you?' Cal shook his head. The beads woven into his dry-locks clicked together. 'You didn't complain when I stole Ferocity. Don't you want to eat?'

'That's different,' Jaiyan mumbled. 'Only poor urchins steal food.'

Cal squeezed his brother's hand. He shared Jaiyan's pride, but admitting to it wouldn't win this argument. 'We won't be poor urchins once we see the emperor.'

'I don't like the emperor.'

'You don't like anyone.'

Jaiyan did have a point. The military hadn't turned against their family's clan without orders from *somebody* important. But none of that mattered now. All Cal cared about was himself, his brother, and the means by which they'd look after themselves. Besides, their blood was Dra'bish. They were proud of a good trade, and being able to sense when someone was disingenuous. The emperor would hand over his fortune in exchange for the sword, and as he did so, Cal would look him straight in the eye and smile.

'Cal! Use your gates,' Jaiyan moaned. 'Why do we have to *walk* to Lexura?'

'I can't open a gate to somewhere I've never been before.'

'Just open one where you can see.' Jaiyan pointed to the far distance. 'Then open another, and another—'

'And have you throw up on me again?' Cal said. 'No. I don't want to drain my nebula. What if we're attacked?'

For once Jaiyan didn't argue. Perhaps in his sullen silence he recalled the raid on their estate, and how without Cal's mental arts, neither of them would have escaped alive.

'Just eat before you starve, idiot.'

Plodding from the horizon, the silhouette of a wagon emerged onto the road. It was pulled by a camel—wealthy merchants could afford horses. What sort were these travellers? Perhaps they were the kind to see a ruby-encrusted sword and think to take it for themselves.

'Wait here.'

'No! Take me with—'

'They've already seen a shape on the road. It'd be suspicious if we both disappeared. Draw their attention—but *don't* make them mad at you. I'll be right back.'

Cal formed a weight in his chest, and a substance, warmer than his blood, spread through his veins. Black mist rose from his skin. Like adrenaline, his nebula compelled him to move.

He traced a finger through the air, and it formed an oval gate of twisting smoke. By his will, it expanded until it was large enough to step through. He repeated the motion, imagining its pair—the opposite gate from which he planned to emerge. This was his bloodline art: the ability to shrink the distance between *here* and *there*. His shortcuts. His easy solution.

Cal turned, to conceal his actions from the wagon, but Jaiyan was clutching at his tunic, trying to stop him from leaving. He sidestepped his brother, and plunged into the nebula. Into the blackness. There was nothing, save for the sensation of falling in the space between stars.

He stumbled onto snow. Cal fought the cold, baring his teeth to the wind; he'd only need to endure it for a few moments. Quickly he retrieved the weapon strapped to his back. Though it was as large as a broadsword, to Cal it weighed almost nothing.

Regalia swords were no ordinary weapons; they carried a will of their own. That's why Cal was certain the emperor would want it. Then they could afford a home in Lexura—somewhere safe from the war.

Ferocity was their future. No wagon bandits could know of it.

He knelt before a stack of iced stones. The wind shrieked in his ears as he dug. This mountain top, high on the southern border of Dra'bah, was Cal's new favourite place to escape to—or hide something. The ridges were sheer and sleek, and save for the tallest plateaus, were enveloped by cloudy fog. No one lived in these peaks, and only someone as determined and desperate as Cal would ever climb to these parts. He'd done so a few months ago, precisely to have access to a remote location via his gates.

Cal hated to part with the sword. Leaving it out of sight for too long strained his nerves. He admired the vibrant rubies set into its steel, which formed a pattern of flames down the blade. To make sure their gleam was hidden he packed snow tightly around it. He buried Ferocity, reassured that the centuries-old sword could never rust nor dull.

With the sword concealed, Cal pulsed his nebula, redrew his gates and stepped back through the dark smoke.

He expected to emerge into sunlight. Instead, he stepped into the shade of an unknown wagon. Flicking snow from his tunic, Cal waited for his body to thaw in the sudden heat of the desert. The camel at the wagon's front snorted at his appearance, but thankfully no one else seemed to notice. Hearing voices on the other side of the wagon, Cal risked a peek.

Jaiyan was cornered, his small back pressed against a wheel. Two burly travellers rested their hands on sword hilts. They appeared to be Dra'bish, both with the same brown skin as Cal and his brother. But there was an important difference—their hair was light and tawny.

'What clan are you, boy? You're clearly Kurakai,' one man said. He gestured to Jaiyan's midnight black hair, which marked all who carried nebula in their veins. 'Why not come with us? I'm sure your clan will pay for your safe return.'

'I have no clan,' Jaiyan protested through sniffles, facing men who wouldn't hesitate to make a slave of him. He was being brave.

'Probably a refugee,' the other man said. 'I've heard both the Rytake and Hyate have nearly wiped themselves out.'

'Are you a warrior, son?' the first man asked. 'Could you make yourself useful?'

They'd regret thinking of Kurakai as tools. Cal removed a small dagger from his belt and, still hidden from view, drew a new gate. Black mist encircled his arms at the same time it coalesced behind the men. Cal saw Jaiyan stiffen.

Cal stepped through—and emerging knife first, buried it into the windpipe of a thug. The man gurgled on his blood in surprise.

Cal wrenched the dagger free and whirled on the second man who fumbled for his sword.

'Kurakai assassin!' he hollered, though there was no one left to help him.

Nebula pulsing, Cal moved with greater strength and speed than this man—than any *common* Numulai—could ever dream of matching. Cal punched his dagger into the man's chest. The strength behind his blow cracked the man's ribs and caved in his chest.

---

In the days that followed, Cal and Jaiyan rode together on the camel they'd stolen from the wagon.

Vegetation asserted itself across the crests and troughs of the terrain, as they left behind the flat expanses of the desert. Soon the king's road was carving its way through Lexura's dense forests which brimmed with the chatter of insects and the beating of parrot wings.

Cal held the reins, and Jaiyan sat tucked in front of him, sniffling constantly. For all the fuss his brother had made about the stolen fruit, he'd not said a word in the aftermath of the fight. He knew Cal had to do it to protect them. Cal was a trained Kurakai, wasn't he? Being a warrior was in his blood. Killing was his duty.

Not that Jaiyan's crying had ever really been about fruit. He was a child, exhausted from travel, and no doubt missed what had been stolen from them. The death of two opportunistic travellers meant very little compared to the war they'd left behind.

By the second day, signs of civilisation returned. Farmhouses, waystations, and inns dotted the roadside, which soon became paved with cobbles.

That eve, they made it to the empire's capital.

Jaiyan slept, slumped against Cal's arms and chest, and missed the great arch bridge rise into view. Cal hadn't been aware bridges could be built so large. Shimmering in the gentle glow of lanterns, the capital sprawled across two hills, one on either side of the Ferryway river. On the eastern peak stood the Observatory of Prosperity. On the inland rise crested the emperor's palace. But Cal hadn't come to sightsee. He'd come to sell the emperor a Regalia sword.

They took the longer route to the upper city, as many of the roads were blocked by soldiers to allow the wagon trains of clan masters uninterrupted passage to the palace. Soon he was forced to jostle Jaiyan awake, help him down, and abandon the aging camel. Despite the pangs in his stomach, he ignored the cries of vendors, and the apple-berry jam and whalebone broth that was shoved in their faces.

Built in the old Kurakai tradition, the palace was three tiers of snow gum timber. Curved pagoda eaves pointed upwards, and all was surrounded by a high wall. It was as formidable as it was elegant. Not that Cal, who had his shortcuts, had ever been bothered by walls or doors.

He led Jaiyan to the guarded entrance. Before them loomed a gate as high as the palace roof, square-cut and painted a brilliant white. Four soldiers were at rest, spears at their sides. They appeared warm in their white military coats and hakama trousers. On their heads, they wore thick, ushanka caps, braced down over their ears. He'd heard rumours that it snowed in Lexura city, but Cal wouldn't believe it until he saw it for himself.

The guards were pale-skinned, and he supposed that was the norm in Lexura. Their stances were at ease, but if they were anything like the Dra'bish redcoats, these soldiers would be just as battle-ready. Though judging by their black hair, each was distinctly Kurakai.

'Move along,' a female whitecoat ordered, waving a dismissive hand at Cal.

The cold welcome wasn't a surprise; he'd expected they'd try and turn them away. But since nobody here knew about his mental arts, Cal thought he'd at least try and ask first.

'I need to see Emperor Damon,' he said.

'We'll let him know you dropped by.' The soldiers exchanged smirks.

'Is this the palace?' Jaiyan asked, rubbing his eyes. The boy's sleepy murmur drew the female whitecoat's attention. She scrutinized Jaiyan and seemed to take pity.

'You're both Kurakai? You don't seem to be urchins.' She looked to the bulkiest soldier—perhaps the commander—distinguished by his open-faced helm which sprouted white feathers. 'Should we fetch someone? They may be blood relatives to the visiting clans.' She eyed their dirt-smeared skin and ragged tunics, and hedged, 'or aides to their retinues, perhaps.'

'No exemptions granted while the palace hosts the Assembly,' the commander grunted. 'Clear them away.'

Cal eyed the steps to the palace main hall, which was at the far end of the inner mounting yard. Stable hands and soldiers milled about, organising the surplus of horses and wagons from the visiting clans.

He drew his first gate. Cal traced its outline again, and the second appeared at the foot of the steps as a swirling oval of mist. Guards shouted in alarm, and Cal suppressed a smile. Even in the city, it seemed no Kurakai had an ability quite like his.

He grabbed Jaiyan by the hand and tugged him into the emptiness between spaces. Their next step saw them emerge at the hall's entry. He yanked Jaiyan out of the nebula, then scattered the mist away with a clench of his fist.

Two sentries levelled their spears, and the sound of racing boots announced more coming. Yelling echoed from behind. By the main gate, it seemed the soldiers were still trying to comprehend how the two boys—who'd stood before them moments before—were now inside the palace walls.

Cal had a clear view of the main corridor inside. He chose his next target and drew. Seeing black smoke rise from his hands, the whitecoats braced, as if expecting an attack. Instead, Cal and Jaiyan stepped into the mist.

They surfaced at the far end of a grand hall. He ignored the mounting nausea in his belly and quickly closed his gates so no soldiers could follow. Jaiyan was clutching Cal's arm to keep his wobbly legs from collapsing. He was proud of how well Jaiyan endured rapid gate hopping, for he was not as immune to its effects as Cal was.

He spied a balcony corridor above. If he was emperor, would he make his chambers on the highest level? Shouts from more guards made Cal's decision for him. He drew his next set and stepped through.

Emerging on the level above, he was almost skewered by a roaring whitecoat aiming a pike tip for his gut. He summoned nebula to his core just in time to block the blow. The tip pierced his tunic but skittered off his skin, as if deflected by a shield—skin could not be penetrated where nebula flowed.

Off-balance, Cal drew again, and haphazardly guessed the position for its pair on the next balcony over. He shoved himself and Jaiyan through.

Jaiyan tumbled to the timber planks and vomited. Cal suspected his brother couldn't handle many more hops through the void. He stood, feeling unsteady on his own feet. Through his spinning vision, he forced himself to focus.

Find Emperor Damon. Show him the sword. Then he'd call off his pack of nipping whitecoats. After that, he'd have no choice but to treat Cal with the respect he deserved.

He spotted a far stairwell, which appeared to lead upwards to the final tier. Guards hollered, their volume increasing as they drew nearer.

Another gate. More darkness. The cold shiver that accompanied it.

He stepped forward, expecting to exit—and his foot met nothing. Cal's stomach lurched. He didn't know what would happen to them if he closed the gates before making it out the other side, and he'd never wanted to find out.

Cal didn't stop tugging his brother's hand until they were both safely through.

'Please, Cal. Not again. Don't make me—' Jaiyan dry retched, interrupting his whimpers.

'I told you you'd throw up,' Cal said. 'But we're almost there. I promise.'

He dragged Jaiyan up the stairs. Sweat matted his dry-locks and his limbs were heavy and numb—signs that Cal was reaching the limits of his nebula use.

They made it to the landing.

A spear shaft struck Cal in the back of the knee, then he received a second strike to his skull. He collapsed, belatedly pulsing to protect from more strikes. Hands seized his limbs and he was pressed face-first to the stone floor. He writhed, but by their sheer number, whitecoats kept him down. Cal stopped fighting, choosing to save the last of his nebula reserves. He'd fall unconscious if he used it all. Instead he accepted their frustrated fists—to his ribs, to his back—as they made sure he wouldn't try anything more.

Somewhere behind him, Jaiyan was crying again, and the sound pierced his chest. Cal could endure this, but he wouldn't let them hurt his brother.

'How did they make it this far?' one soldier demanded of another. 'The clan masters and their families are on this floor!'

'The older one, his mental art is potent,' another panted. 'He moves through these ... portals. A Hyate, maybe?'

'Impossible. There are no Hyate left.'

Cal twisted so he could speak. 'I have a weapon to sell to the emperor—' An elbow struck his side and he gasped.

'You dare speak of the Emperor of Toraq,' a soldier growled. 'Get 'em up. Take them to the lower level.'

---

At spear point, Cal and Jaiyan were led down several staircases, until they reached the foundations of the palace. Despite his blurry vision and heavy bones, Cal cooperated with the whitecoats. He was not willing to lose his chance to speak to the emperor.

When they reached a fork in the corridor, Cal assumed they'd be shuffled right, towards what looked like the dungeons. Instead they were shoved left towards an armoury. Whatever they were playing at, he didn't like it.

They were made to stand before a large workbench. Behind them loomed rows of shelves stacked with the tonfa, naginata, spears and swords of the empire's military. His brother pressed to his side, and though this embarrassed Cal, he was at least grateful that Jaiyan had stopped crying.

The soldiers had exited, leaving them alone with a single guard. The guard appeared to be sixteen, was of dark complexion, and stole endless glances towards the door. He was Kurakai, judging by the fact he'd been trusted to remain on his own, as well as the dark tangle of hair which curled over the rim of his spectacles. He'd introduced himself as Tyron, the armourer's apprentice, but had said nothing more thereafter. By his nervous fidgeting, he was just as perplexed to be there as Cal and Jaiyan.

'Why are we here, not the dungeons?' Cal demanded. 'What do they want with us?'

Tyron jumped at the sudden question. 'Truly, I don't know why he'd show personal interest,' he mumbled. 'Perhaps because you are Dra'bish.' Tyron indicated to his desert-red uniform and gave a small smile of comradery. 'As am I.'

'You're a traitor to your clan, is what you are,' Cal said, causing Tyron to pale.

The door rattled and opened. Sentries entered and offered obeisance as a new figure strode into the armoury. Broad-shouldered and half-a-head taller than the guards, this man loomed without needing to adjust his posture. Hands behind back, he stood like a soldier at parade rest. He too wore the military uniform—the high-neck, side-buttoned coat and hakama—except his was emerald green. Cal recognised what that colour meant, even without the bowing and averted eyes of the soldiers.

Cal tried to read the emperor's guarded expression. Was he curious, or amused? He wasn't that old, but the streaks of grey in his hair made him *seem* older. Cal wasn't even aware a Kurakai's black hair could grey with age.

'Word has reached me of two new guests,' the emperor said, examining Cal and Jaiyan. 'We'd not prepared for a Hyate delegation to join us.'

Tyron laughed nervously at the emperor's joke.

One last person stepped into the armoury. A boy, similar to Cal's own age, or perhaps a year older, gave them no acknowledgement at all. He folded himself into a corner, crossed his arms and fixed his scowl on a point in the distance. His curls were cropped so short they spiked out at odd angles. He looked remarkably similar to Tyron, and Cal guessed the two were related. But why this second boy was here, he'd no idea.

'Your name?' the emperor commanded of Cal.

'Hyate Calcifer,' he said, parting with his full name. A short silence followed.

'You really are Hyate?' Tyron asked, with what sounded like academic curiosity. 'How did you survive what happened to your clan?'

The emperor interrupted. 'You doubt the boy's claim? Didn't you hear the guards describe his mental arts?' The emperor invited Cal forwards with a gesture. 'I'd see your abilities for myself.'

Cal stiffened. 'I'm not here to perform. I've come to barter.'

'That's right. This talk of a weapon,' he mused. 'Well then, little Dra'bish merchant. Go and get it.'

The emperor leaned against the bench, giving Cal the distinct impression he was being humoured. Cal flushed, realising he'd stepped into a trick. Ferocity was still on the snowy peak where he'd left it, and to retrieve the sword, Cal would need to use his nebula gates. The emperor would get his performance regardless. Just as tinder sparked, so did Cal's hate.

Shoving his exhaustion aside, he untangled his arm from Jaiyan's white-knuckled grip. Testing his reserves, it seemed he'd have enough nebula left to play this game. Beneath scrutinising stares, he affixed the peak in his mind and drew his first gate.

Cal strode through the black mist.

Immediately lashed by a bone-deep chill, he hurried to uncover Ferocity. Relief washed through him as he grasped the cold hilt. The sword thrummed encouragingly as he dusted snow off its blade. Then he pulsed and drew his path back. Purposely, he aimed to re-emerge *behind* his three adjudicators.

The warm air of the armoury was welcoming. Tyron gave a startled squawk as Cal stepped out behind them. With a shrug, Cal brushed the last snow flecks from his tunic.

'Ferocity,' Cal said. 'One of the five Regalia swords.'

The emperor watched Cal with careful, grey eyes. Then he nodded to one of the whitecoat guards by the door. 'You. Demonstrate with the sword. Give it a testing swing.'

The solider strode forward with purpose, and Cal held the weapon flat on both palms. Though longer and wider than his arms, it weighed nothing at all. He allowed the soldier to take it, and fought back a smirk.

The moment Ferocity was in the man's grip, the sword rebelled. It was fumbled, dropped and sliced open the soldier's forearm. Tyron gasped and rushed to assist the guard's bleeding wound. The sleeve of his white coat was already soaked red.

'Incredible,' the emperor mused. 'She resisted you immediately. Fighting back with a will of her own.' He looked to Tyron. 'Your turn.'

Tyron paled further.

Cal retrieved Ferocity, thoroughly unconcerned by its tumble to the stone. A Regalia sword could not be damaged so easily. He held it out to the armourer's apprentice.

'You're Dra'bish, like me,' Cal said, indicating to Tyron's red uniform. 'Ferocity only attacked him because he's Lexuran. But to us—she'll answer to our blood.'

Tyron still appeared unwilling.

'I'll do it.' The younger boy in military red shoved towards them. 'It's probably a fake. That oaf has always been a clumsy fool.'

Was he calling Cal a liar? He glared and the boy glared back.

'Go on,' the emperor encouraged. 'This is Lyncoln Thorn. If the sword is as you say, it'll answer to him as well.'

Cal didn't want to give this boy Ferocity, but his trade may depend on it. He handed over the sword.

Thorn weighed Ferocity and frowned. He whirled the blade over deftly, and it bothered Cal how well he suited the weapon. Thorn's frown deepened.

'Describe how it feels,' the emperor prompted.

'It's light, for its bulk,' Thorn muttered, turning it over. 'And it ... vibrates. As if eager to be used.' Thorn shook his head and placed Ferocity on the workbench.

The emperor nodded. 'That appears to be her, as she is described by legend. It's a boon for the empire to have a Regalia sword back in the Assembly's care. Tyron, see it locked away securely.'

Cal opened his mouth, but Jaiyan's shrill voice struck first.

'You need to pay us for it!' his brother shouted. 'Otherwise it's stealing!'

The emperor smiled thinly. 'And how am I to believe two young orphans, dressed in rags, who broke into my palace, obtained this relic in the first place? This artefact is priceless for its cultural and historical significance. I've no choice but to see it confiscated.'

As he spoke, Cal calmly drew a small gate, just wide enough to fit his arm through. Its pair appeared beside Ferocity's hilt. Cal reached through, arm appearing on the opposite side of the bench. Thorn started in alarm.

Cal pulled Ferocity back through. Sword safely in his possession—and before anyone could stop him—he summoned more gates. Opening a passage to the snowy peak, Cal tossed the sword through. Jaiyan grabbed Cal's sleeve, not in fear, but in a smug show of: *see what my brother can do?*

Everyone stared at him. Expressions ranged from incredulity, scowls, and in the emperor's case, impressed satisfaction.

'Ferocity stays with me,' Cal said, 'until you make an offer I agree to.'

'Such false cleverness your arts have imbued you with.' The emperor nodded slowly, then gestured to the whitecoats by the entry. They held their spears in semi-ready grips, seemingly uncertain if there was danger to protect against.

'See these boys looked after and tidied. Hyate Calcifer is to dine with me this evening.'

---

Cal did not like the silk robes provided by the palace staff. He liked it even less when they separated him from his brother. But he obeyed, knowing it unlikely he'd be granted his audience with the emperor until he discarded the ruined clothes he'd travelled in.

He knelt on a cushion, fiddling with the hem of the sash around his middle. Before him, a low table offered a spread of turtle and yabbie meat presented in their shells. Everything was drizzled in the juices of strawberry gum and white elderberry.

Kneeling opposite him was the emperor. Removed from his emerald uniform, he was now dressed in a robe likely considered low for his station, and wore no ornaments to mark his position as the military's supreme commander. His only trinket was a necklace, from which hung a grey river stone. He insisted Cal address him as 'Master Damon'.

To Cal's right sat Thorn. The boy hadn't looked at him since the meal began, yet he still radiated condescension. He ground every mouthful with a grudge.

Cal knew his type, no doubt born to the wealthy branch of his clan. Perhaps he was even the son of a clan master. Though Ferocity proved he was Dra'bish, he'd clearly not been raised there, nor experienced the war. Thorn and Damon both looked the same as Cal, yet neither tied their hair in the traditional dry-locks, nor wore their beads. They'd been in the capital too long.

Cal picked at his meal, too tired to be hungry, and not certain he could stomach this Lexuran food. In fact, the entirety of the emperor's guest-chamber—from the tightly woven straw mats to the fine tapestries of the constellations—turned Cal from his appetite. His head still ached from the staff strike, so he ate just enough to seem polite.

'Thirteen,' Damon repeated, having pried Cal's age from him earlier in the conversation. 'It is remarkable to be so proficient in the mental arts at your age.'

Cal dug at his yabbie shell to keep from answering.

'Has your brother manifested a similar art? To these gates?'

'No,' Cal lied, and wondered if he'd answered too quickly. His heart pounded. 'Jaiyan is untrained both in the physical and mental arts.'

'And yet you are unusually adept in both.'

'My clan needed warriors.' He dared not say more. If the rumours were to be believed, it was this man across from him who'd begun the war in his kingdom: who'd ordered the extinction of his bloodline. He balled his fists in his lap.

'There is a reason why I could not introduce Lyncoln Thorn to you as my apprentice,' Damon continued, dusting lemon myrtle into a shell. 'Perhaps you're aware. Tradition demands the ruler of this empire take two apprentices. If I do not adhere to this, I risk angering the clans further.' From the way he spoke, Damon did not seem concerned by this at all. 'I plan to bury the barbaric Coronation duel, and simply choose, on merit, my own successor. But Thorn's formal instruction cannot begin until I choose another to train alongside him. The clans parade their offspring before me, hoping that one of their blood may one day rule Toraq.'

Damon looked to Cal and smiled conspiratorially. 'Wouldn't it rankle the clan masters if I were to choose someone else? A Kurakai child they've never heard of, from a clan thought dead and unimportant?'

The yabbie shell in Cal's hands cracked. It now made sense why Thorn had seemingly wanted to stab Cal from the moment the meal had begun. The emperor wanted a second heir. By tradition, Thorn needed a competitor.

Cal tried to imagine himself as an emperor's apprentice and was dizzied and ashamed all at once. Would his parents be proud or mortified? He didn't know.

'You don't want me,' Cal said. 'You want to use my abilities.'

'That's true,' Damon conceded. 'But, moreso, I wish to avoid selecting a child from the wealthy clans. Tradition has held this empire back for too long.'

Thorn's nebula flared and the eating sticks in his fist snapped.

'*You* should be celebrating,' Damon chided Thorn. 'From here, I can formally recognise you as my apprentice. If I've made a mistake by choosing Calcifer, if he fails to impress, then be pleased that the empire will someday be yours.'

'Yes, master,' Thorn muttered.

'And you,' Damon returned his stare to Cal, 'no matter the outcome, can secure a future far more comfortable, for you and your brother, than any coin a stolen sword could bring.'

Had Cal's plan really been that easy to read? He hated the emperor's ability to stare straight through him.

'And if I say no? You can't keep me here,' Cal said.

'Get in, get out; is that your style, young Calcifer?' Damon mused. 'Aren't you old enough to appreciate delayed gratification? What exactly does your future hold? As someone in your position who has experienced, what I can only imagine has been, trying circumstances.'

Damon fixed him with a grin like a curved blade. 'You can't go back and change what has happened, but perhaps, one day, you may have the influence—the power—to prevent that from happening to you, or your brother, ever again. Leaving now may bring fleeting benefits. But stay, and the rewards will be far greater.'

It felt like walls were closing in around him. Cal refused to be trapped by walls.

'I'm keeping Ferocity,' he said, but sounded more petulant than he'd hoped.

'I suppose you will. The empire will not barter for such an artefact,' Damon said. 'Any merchant discovered auctioning a Regalia sword will face severe repercussions.'

'You'll make it impossible for me to sell it?' Cal accused, voice rising. 'I don't need a master. What more could you teach me?'

Thorn made a noise and Cal turned to glare at him. But Thorn's expression wasn't hostile; it was astonished. Only then did Cal realise he'd said something extremely stupid.

'I have ended wars,' Damon said carefully. 'You couldn't even save your family. There is much I could teach you. You came here to trade, didn't you? In that case, I counsel greater investment for greater returns. That is the deal I offer.'

Cal hated the heat rising in his cheeks. Damon was patronising him. The emperor didn't care about Ferocity, and his earlier claim about 'historical significance' had clearly been a bluff. Cal, and his mental arts, were the only prize he sought.

Yet, somewhere in this palace, Jaiyan was warmer, cleaner and more well-fed than he'd been in months. As the brother to an emperor's apprentice, Jaiyan would be protected by the military—not on the run from them. Better still, as an emperor's apprentice, Cal would become strong enough to protect him all on his own.

'I need time,' Cal said hoarsely.

Damon nodded. 'I expect an answer by tomorrow.'

Jaiyan was curled up asleep in a futon by the time Cal returned to their assigned chambers. Cal adjusted Jaiyan's blankets, making sure he was warm. At least he finally had the soft bed Cal had promised him all these months.

Despite his aches, Cal was too tense to unroll his own futon.

He wandered the palace balconies, drawing stares from the soldiers on night watch. But none tried to stop him. Navigating to the palace centre, he stumbled across a garden.

Firewheels, waratahs, scarlet princesses and bottlebrushes grew side by side—a native flower from each of the four kingdoms, and nothing but a shallow demonstration of the empire's unity. Just as the emperor's proposal over dinner had been no true offer of apprenticeship. It wasn't as if Cal would ever become emperor. The clan warlords would never unite behind a street urchin from a dead bloodline. Thorn had been groomed to rule from birth, and Damon had taken him under his wing long before he'd ever known Cal existed. Thorn was clearly the chosen successor.

Yet even as the 'spare', Cal would be forced to call Damon his master. The emperor would have the power to command Cal's abilities for his own ends. In exchange for safety and comfort, Cal would be giving up his freedom: the ability to go wherever, whenever he wanted, with a single step.

Forget bartering. Cal and Jaiyan had survived worse. They could leave this city and find another way.

Something struck Cal's spine. His instincts flared before he felt the pain. He pulsed nebula and whirled—and the staff struck under his chin. His vision blotted and he fell prone into the garden bed. A small rock dug into his back.

Hoping he had enough nebula left, he reached to draw a gate.

'No, you don't.'

The staff clapped against his wrist with nebula strength, and Cal cried out.

Thorn stood above him, wearing a satisfied smirk. The blunt end of the staff was poised above Cal's chest.

'Pathetic,' Thorn said. 'And you called yourself a warrior. I train for this my entire life, and you show up and expect to be treated as my equal? Damon is losing his mind if he believes I'd ever call an orphan nobody my apprentice-brother.'

Cal turned his wrist over, testing that the bone wasn't broken. With his other hand, he felt for the jagged stone hidden under his back as Thorn spoke on.

'You should be grateful he abolished the Coronation duel. Do you even know what that was? A fight to the death was how we use to choose Toraq's ruler. You would have been no challenge to me at all.'

'I know about Coronation,' Cal muttered. Despite what Thorn thought of him, he hadn't been born under a rock. Every Kurakai knew the tales of those fights. Damon had notoriously bowed out of his, and had acknowledged his apprentice-brother as king—only to stab his friend in the back decades later and declare himself an emperor.

Cal supposed he could respect a good feint.

He lunged with the rock. Thorn sidestepped and tripped Cal with the staff. At the same time, the rock tugged free from his grasp as if by unseen hands. Encompassed by nebula, the rock flew into Thorn's outstretched palm. In a burst of black mist, Thorn crushed the rock to pieces.

'You're not the only one with mental arts, Hyate,' Thorn sneered. 'You have no respect for rank. Learn your place.'

Thorn struck again, but this time Cal was ready. Nebula pulsing, he caught the staff and held on. He was pleased to discover he had several inches height over Thorn, despite the age difference.

'To the wastes with you,' Thorn hissed as they struggled over the staff. 'Why do you even want him as your master? He's an honourless bastard. Who do you think ordered the Hyate massacre?'

Cal knew the rumours. But he'd never wasted time wondering who'd decreed *this* or *that* when he'd been more concerned with where Jaiyan's next meal would come from.

But hearing it confirmed, from *Thorn* no less, stung deeply. He relinquished the staff.

'Wouldn't you prefer an orphan nobody to compete against?' Cal bit back. 'Damon all but said you'll be emperor someday. He just needs me as the spare.'

Thorn snapped the staff to attention, looking every bit a bastard redcoat soldier. 'Only the best competition is good enough for me. If Damon won't respect the old traditions, then someone around here must,' Thorn said. With a final sneer, he turned his back and left.

Cal shook his wrist again, annoyed at how much it still hurt. Thorn had snuck up on him—in the dark—and now thought he was the better warrior for it?

He'd been so close to leaving, determined that no one would force him to become like the soldiers who'd stormed his home. He'd been moments away from waking Jaiyan, drawing a gate and vanishing before morning.

But that would have been the easy solution. The shortcut. He'd be leaving that spoiled brat to one day rule, or perhaps someone worse. Someone who'd continue to obliterate the defiant clans.

Cal was being given the opportunity to be a different kind of redcoat. *Greater investment, greater returns.*

Thorn wanted the best competition, did he? Someone who could genuinely impress Damon, and potentially be named emperor one day?

Lucky for him, Thorn already had his answer.

---

The Assembly was summoned for the emperor to make the formal announcement, and by mid-next morning, Cal was presented with his own military uniform. The coat was Dra'bish desert-red, in honour of his home kingdom. He refused to comb out his dry-locks as they'd asked. As a compromise, he tied his beads and braids back into a tail. Jaiyan had laughed at him and said he looked stupid. Cal felt stupid. But at least his brother was smiling.

On his way to the Assembly, he'd caught his reflection in the polished armour of his escort. The green eyes that stared back were still his own, but everything else was foreign. Cal's reflection now instilled in him the same fight-or-flight response he'd honed against all redcoats. Men who'd worn this uniform had slaughtered his clan.

Now he was one of them.

In a crowded half-moon amphitheatre, the emperor presented his two apprentices to the Assembly. Thorn was introduced first, as the son of the late king and high priestess.

Cal blinked. He hadn't known that. Should he have known that? Everyone in the empire knew the story of the coup. Damon had become Toraq's first emperor after ending the line of kings. But the last king had sons.

*Stars*, was Thorn an actual prince?

Cal was introduced simply as Hyate Calcifer, parents unmentioned.

The Numulai officials and the clan masters received the news in stunned silence. Cal was pleased to see Thorn bristle. The *prince* seemed annoyed to be placed on equal standing as him, and to be seen in matching uniforms.

After the ceremony, palace staff presented cups of blue gum wine in the gardens, as well as trays of desert figs and roasted cashews. The clan masters and their families mingled. Cal had been instructed to make himself available.

Soon he understood what Damon had meant when he'd described the clan habit of parading their offspring. Every retinue included at least one young Kurakai, formally dressed, who conversed with the adults as equals. Without fail, each one stared daggers in Cal's direction.

In particular, he noticed the child of the Danore clan. Perhaps fourteen, the girl—addressed as Loretta—received much sympathy and condolences. From what Cal overheard, it seemed the girl had recently lost a younger sister to drowning. When no one else was looking, he received from her the most dire glare of all.

Cal stayed in constant motion to avoid being trapped in conversation. He was briefly introduced to a Kurakai master and mistress, the elegant Adrian and Madix of the Saiake. He was able to slip away, for the mistress was heavily pregnant and had enough well-wishers of her own. Kurakai children were not as common as Numulai, so any new arrival appeared to be an Assembly talking point.

'Calcifer, was it?' A young man asked, striding towards him. Cal fought the urge to open a gate.

'Cal is fine.'

'Kisame Hec'Tor,' he said and bowed. 'Congratulations on your appointment. Please, you must meet my sister.' Hec'Tor waved to a girl. Dressed in a formal robe and sash, black hair neatly pinned, she was the perfect image of a clan master's daughter.

'Vi'Toria, meet Calcifer. Told you I could corner him.'

Vi'Toria stared at Cal. Her eyes widened ... in terror?

'It's *you*,' she whispered. Cal checked over his shoulder, to be certain she was speaking to him.

'Do you know him?' Hec'Tor asked.

'I've *seen* him.'

Cal had no idea what this answer meant, but Hec'Tor appeared to understand. Suddenly his expression was cold.

'We need to speak to mother and father,' she said, tugging on her elder brother's sleeve. She abruptly turned her back on Cal, just like every other estate Kurakai had done so, when he and Jaiyan had shown up dirty and cold.

Cal was irrationally angry. This is what he'd expected: to be looked down upon by the wealthy clans. But he shouldn't have to make himself *available* to receive the treatment.

He stomped further into the gardens, eager to find a moment alone.

'Don't take it personally. Vi'Toria's not so bad,' called an amused voice.

He turned and found another Kurakai youth kneeling by a pond. She was older than him, and wore no shoes. Her dark hair was around her shoulders, and slightly unkempt. A sincere lack of effort had been applied to her robes.

'You mean she's not a bitch?'

She gave him a chiding tilt of her head. 'No, she just has a lot on her mind. The Kisame are a powerful clan, and are the emperor's most vocal opponents. How would you feel if your parents were on the brink of starting a war?'

Cal stared at her. She instantly went red.

'Sorry, I forgot you were Hyate.' She stood, offered out a flat palm and introduced herself as Cyliya Clarissia. 'Call me Rissa.'

Cal placed his palm on top of hers, then returned his hands to his pockets. 'After what happened in Dra'bah, you'd think the clans would quiet down.'

'I'd say things are worse.' Rissa shrugged. 'No clan approves of Damon's foreign beloved. Now he chooses an arbitrary apprentice to spite everyone? No offence meant. But everyone is going to hate you.'

At least Cal would be used to it. Rissa lowered her voice to a whisper, and nodded over his shoulder.

'That's the girl you need to look out for.'

Cal followed her gaze. She indicated to the girl named Loretta, the one with the predator's gaze and hair pulled back into a severe, high tail. She was deep in conversation with Thorn, as the two sat on a stone bench. At least, *Thorn* was sitting on the bench. Loretta was in his lap. Thorn was neither encouraging her, nor pushing her away.

'Her clan wanted her for Damon's apprentice. Ever since her sister died, their efforts have become far more ... aggressive.'

'I don't think what she has in mind for Thorn is an apprentice brother-sister relationship,' Cal said, drawing a giggle from Rissa. 'What about you?' he asked, emboldened. 'Do I need to look out for you?'

'If you wish to,' she answered, and it was his turn to redden. Of all the clan heirs present, Rissa was the first to seem like a real person. 'I would've been a poor choice,' she said. 'I'm no warrior, and my mental arts are drearily simple.' She reached out and gripped Cal's arm. There was a crackling sound, and a sudden shock vibrated through his skeleton.

'Hey!' he said, jumping away. He rubbed at the tingling point on his arm.

'My mother can call the storms. I can make people jump, at best.' She grinned, and Cal couldn't help but return it. She sat back down by the pond. 'No, I never wanted to be Damon's. To be apprenticed to any master ... it never felt right. I already know I'll keep my own children from it.'

Finding a dry patch of ground, Cal joined her by the pool.

'I'm only here for the food,' he said honestly. 'And the palace futons. Everyone here has secrets and weird motives. I don't want anything to do with that.'

'You won't have a choice,' Rissa countered. 'For all the clans who see Damon as a usurper, he also has his followers. And those clans aren't going to support Thorn—the son of the former king. No, they'll rally behind the alternative.' She gave Cal a sidelong glance. 'That's you, now. Training your nebula is only half of the apprenticeship. Like it or not, you'll have to become a leader.'

Their conversation trailed off as a tall woman approached.

'Were you listening to everything?' Rissa complained, then muttered to Cal, 'Cyliya Iris, my mother, and mistress of our clan.'

Cal stood and offered his obeisance. The woman's gaze was astute, and Cal shrank beneath it.

'And are you to be our next emperor?' Iris asked, voice as smooth as water.

'That's for Damon to decide.'

'Nonsense,' Iris dismissed. 'The Elders among the stars have always chosen our ruler. If Damon denies them a Coronation, they will find other ways to make their will known.'

Since the murder of his family, he hadn't felt particularly 'Elders-blessed'. Cal couldn't imagine the Elders ever wanting him to represent them.

But Rissa and Iris had made something clear, something that Cal had not fully grasped until now. It made little sense for Damon to truly want the son of the king he usurped to become his successor. Perhaps there was a reason the emperor had taken so long to choose his next apprentice: Cal wasn't to be the spare. Thorn was secondary to *him*.

Cal gripped Ferocity and felt its thrum. Thorn stood across the raked sands of the training yard, armed with his spear. There was no hiding how impatient they were to humiliate one another.

They'd rejected training weapons, as they were both experienced in nebula blocking. Thorn, in his bravado, announced he was eager for Cal to use Ferocity against him, despite knowing a Regalia sword could slice through nebula. Cal, reassured there was a Lyrissia healer somewhere nearby, had no qualms. After a nod from their master, Cal had retrieved the sword.

At Damon's command, they lunged.

With a flick of his wrist, Cal summoned a gate to his left. Narrowly avoiding Thorn's spear point, he sank through his gate and emerged behind him. Cal lashed—and though the sword readily responded, Cal misjudged the distance. The large blade swung and Thorn easily sidestepped.

They drove each other to exhaustion and madness, neither managing to land a blow. No matter how fast Thorn moved, he could never catch Cal before he vanished through a gate—and as thrilling as it was to wield Ferocity, Cal was unfamiliar with the unnaturally large sword and was struggling to adapt.

'Enough!' Damon yelled, ending the fight. Cal dropped to his knees to catch his breath. The sand shifted behind him, and from the corner of his eye, Cal saw a spear tip flash. He was too sluggish to move in time ...

The emperor reacted. In a burst of speed, Damon caught the spear point Thorn was driving towards Cal's back. Damon yanked the weapon from Thorn's grip.

'The fight was done!' Damon shouted.

'He doesn't deserve that sword!' Thorn yelled back. 'He doesn't deserve to be here! He's nothing but dirt!'

With nebula strength, Damon slapped Thorn. His cheek crunched, and Thorn was driven into the sand. The boy gurgled and spat blood.

Cal shook. Thorn had tried to skewer him in the back—and he'd almost succeeded. But that's not what had Cal's adrenaline pulsing.

Damon's response had been brutal. These past few weeks Cal was starting to witness the mood swings whispered of around the palace. But most alarming of all: this was the first time Cal had seen Damon's nebula. He'd used it for speed and strength against Thorn, and the mist was still gently rising from his skin.

Damon's nebula wasn't black.

'Why is it silver?' Cal croaked.

Damon gave him an annoyed glance.

'Why is your nebula silver?' Cal repeated, wanting an answer. He'd never heard of such a thing. All Kurakai, with their dark hair, pulsed dark nebula through their veins. What did silver mean? What *was* he?

'Thorn is right,' Damon snapped. 'That sword is wasted on you.'

Protectively, Cal gripped Ferocity's hilt.

'Your entire style relies on sneaking inside an opponent's defences. You get in close and take your enemies by surprise—not by sheer force, as Thorn does.'

Damon nudged Thorn with his boot. The prince was nursing his bloodied cheek, looking at neither Damon nor Cal.

'Try with this,' Damon said, unsheathing the sword from his hip. It was a narrow, elegant blade with a gentle curve, and was only sharp along one edge. It was a Kurakai blade, designed for speed and slicing. Cal never used one like it before.

'I won't give up Ferocity,' he said. 'If this is a trick to make me give it to you—'

'You asked what I could teach you?' Damon asked, and trapped Cal beneath his piercing grey stare. 'Hear this, Calcifer. It is the Swordarm that matters, not the sword. As my apprentice, you will not embarrass me by pursuing an inferior style. Nor will you go your entire life relying solely on shortcuts.'

Damon tossed the single-edge sword, and it fell into the sand at Cal's feet.

'Ferocity, a sword that answers to your will, is just another crutch. A leader must stand on their own two feet.'

---

Cal sifted the snow and replaced Ferocity—*his* sword—back into its hiding place. He shivered but did not rise from his knees. He liked the solitude of this mountain peak, away from the chaos and noise of the palace.

The plan had been to sell this sword, and with that wealth, secure food, safety and all the things he and Jaiyan would ever need. But he knew how this world worked. His hope of escaping the military, one way or another, had been foolish. Instead, he should be proud. After all, Cal had accomplished what he'd set out to do. Never before had they lived in such comfort and wealth.

If only he felt safe.

Cal stood and flexed his nebula-numbed fingers. With a kick of snow he concealed Ferocity's bright rubies, and he suppressed the unease that plucked at him every time he parted with the sword. He drew his gates and returned to the training yard.

The sun was setting, and both his master and apprentice-brother were long gone. With Damon's approval, Thorn had sought out the mistress healer to see to his shattered cheekbone.

'You have lovely green eyes.' A young woman's voice.

Cal whirled, hairs pricked on the back of his neck. He'd thought himself alone.

The girl with the predator's eyes and long hair—Loretta—stood a few paces away, hands behind her back. Cal was tall for his age, but Loretta was easily his same height.

'What do you want?' Cal asked.

She smiled and drew closer. 'I heard Thorn was injured today.'

'That wasn't my fault.'

'I never said it was.'

Her nebula pulsed and her speed was inhuman. Cal gasped. White-hot pain pierced his lower ribs. Loretta's hand gripped the hilt of a stiletto embedded in his torso. Black mist rose from her skin.

'No jumping through gates? You didn't even block. You just stood there.' Loretta twisted the blade and Cal doubled over. She caught him, preventing his fall. He knew he should do something, but the pain and shock had his body anchored.

'You shouldn't have stayed. Now my clan wants you dead. I was to be Damon's apprentice, you know? Instead it goes to you, an ill-bred dingo-dog,' she sneered. 'Do you think Thorn will be upset if I rob him of his Coronation right to kill you?'

Cal gripped her wrist, which still held the blade inside him. With his other hand, he drew a gate. It appeared on the ground behind her and he shoved.

Loretta stumbled back, and her foot vanished into the void. She caught herself and jerked away before completely falling through. She yanked her leg out of the mist—and it came back drenched in water.

'Did you just try to drown me?' she gasped, visibly shaking. If only she knew. Half a step further and she'd be at the bottom of the deepest lake Cal had ever swum.

With the blade torn free, he pressed his hand to his side, but that didn't stop the blood. The sand was stained with it. Had she struck something vital? He was gasping, and his vision was dimming at the edges.

'That's cold. You heard them talk about my sister, didn't you?' Loretta said, squeezing the water from her trouser leg. She gave him an appraising look. 'Maybe there is more to you, Hyate. But my clan won't forget this. Every time you see me, I want you to know that I could have done it. Tonight, I could have killed you if I wanted to.'

She stood, and after one last glance at where his gate had been, she left.

Once certain she was gone, Cal collapsed to his knees. Frightened moans escaped him. He summoned his gates, struggling to concentrate on where he wanted to go. Memories of his first day in the palace, in the armoury, clouded his mind. He crawled through the mist.

The fall through time, the void, felt longer than it should. His stomach clenched.

Cal gasped for air and tumbled forwards. He sprawled onto stone, immediately slicking it with his blood. This was the armoury. He tried to get shaking knees beneath him.

A startled gurgle sounded above him.

Tyron, the armourer's apprentice, stood frozen. The sixteen-year-old clutched his books to his chest as if Cal's blood might soil them. His spectacles looked ready to slip from his nose.

'Help me,' Cal choked. 'Please.'

---

Cal's vision began to clear once the mistress healer administered her mental arts. The healer pressed her palms to the wound, and black smoke rose from between her fingers. As a Lyrissia, it was the constellation of her clan that was prayed to for vitality and health. Later, Cal would need to light a candle in the observatory.

His wound began to close—but he was told the scar would be permanent. The healing left him sluggish and hungry.

Tyron hovered nervously, and appeared relieved when Cal sat under his own strength.

'Who should I go to?' Cal asked the older boy.

'For what?'

'To tell them what Loretta did,' he said. 'She stabbed me!'

'Yes, she does that,' Tyron said. 'And the Danore hold grudges. In general, I'd recommend either not provoking her, or defending yourself.'

'She'll just get away with it?'

'We're Kurakai,' Tyron said dully. 'And you're the emperor's apprentice. A great warrior in training, right? Reporting this would only embarrass your master.'

Cal grimaced as the healer helped him remove his torn red coat.

'I hate it here,' he said. 'If it wasn't for Jaiyan, I'd already be gone.'

'I know a thing or two about younger brothers,' Tyron said with an exhausted sigh. Cal stared, and recalled his first impression of Tyron and Thorn, and their resemblance.

'Why *is* your brother such a jerk?' Cal asked.

'I don't know.' Tyron seemed to genuinely consider it. 'If I could've kept him from putting on the red coat, I would have. I hope this place doesn't have the same effect on yours.'

'Jaiyan isn't joining the military.'

Judging by Tyron's expression, Cal had said something absurd.

'It won't be a choice. I'm surprised he hasn't been claimed by a master already. Better off he volunteers before he ends up somewhere he doesn't like.'

That hadn't been the agreement. If Cal did this for Damon, if he endured this, Jaiyan was supposed to be safe.

The healer interrupted, holding out a fresh tunic for Cal to take.

'He doesn't need to be a soldier,' the healer said gently, clearly having listened to their conversation. 'All military recruits are invited to join the healing core, or any administrative branch. Damon is keen to expand his scribes: training more law acolytes and judges.'

'Or researchers, like me,' Tyron said, brightening. 'Now the civil war is dying down, I'll be returning to the library of Dra'bah to complete my studies. Jaiyan can come with me, if you want. I can keep an eye on him for you.'

'He's not going back to Dra'bah. We just got out!'

Cal wasn't used to feeling this helpless. No matter how bad things had gotten, he'd always been able to grab Jaiyan's hand and drag them through a gate. But these weren't physical things—things to outrun—that now threatened to take his brother away.

'Being the big brother sometimes means making the tough decisions, not the easy ones,' Tyron mumbled. 'Especially since, you know, our parents aren't around anymore.' Tyron fidgeted, readjusting his glasses which hadn't been crooked.

Even if Cal and Jaiyan fled, Damon now knew that two Hyate were still alive, and that was Cal's fault. He'd been so eager to show how clever and powerful he was, that he hadn't thought ahead. Because of him, they'd be on the run for the rest of their lives.

Unless Cal chose to stay.

Perhaps Jaiyan would enjoy studying in a library, half an empire away from the palace. As a Redcoat, he'd have nothing to fear from the kingdom they'd fled. Did they even make uniforms in Jaiyan's size?

Cal tugged off his bloodstained tunic and dragged on the fresh one.

'You promise to look after him?' Cal asked.

Tyron hesitated only briefly. 'Of course.'

'Because I can get to Dra'bah much faster than you can flee it.'

Tyron flinched, and Cal was glad to see it. No, Cal wasn't helpless, nor was he an embarrassment. He could protect his brother and he could fight. Thorn's sneak attacks, Damon's brutality and Loretta's knife had only rattled him. Clearly the capital bred a different kind of Kurakai. If Cal was to match them, then he'd need to stay and learn from the best.

'I hate you, Cal! I hate you! I hate you!'

Jaiyan screamed. Repeatedly he thumped his fists against Cal's chest. His eyes were red and puffy, his nose running. He was trying to summon nebula. Feeble wisps pulsed from his hands. But Jaiyan was untrained, and failed to produce any Kurakai strength behind the blows.

Cal took the punches. It was not the first time Jaiyan had told him he hated him.

'You said we'd be safe here! You said!'

'I was stabbed! What if that happened to you? Sending you away is how I keep you safe,' Cal pleaded. 'I need to impress Damon. That's the new plan. But you can't be here, distracting me.'

'To the wastes with you, Cal!'

'No!' He caught Jaiyan's fist. 'Do *not* joke about that. Not you.'

Jaiyan cowered and tried to wriggle free. Cal sighed and let him go.

'Jai, I'm sorry.'

'I don't want to go home!'

'You like to read, don't you?' Cal hated how stupid he sounded. 'You've always wanted to learn how to throw a javelin? They'll teach you that too.'

A loud fist banged against the outside of their chamber door, and they both jumped. The knocking was demanding.

'Just, wait. And stop crying.' Cal waved for Jaiyan to hush.

He opened the door.

Thorn stood on the other side. His shoulders heaved as if he was out of breath from running. He wasn't wearing his military uniform, just regular training leathers.

'What did you do?' Thorn demanded.

'I don't know what you mean.'

'They're ending the Assembly talks early! They're already preparing to leave!'

'Who?'

'The Kisame!' Thorn ran his fingers back through his spikey hair. He was clearly rattled—Cal had never seen him like this before. But the moment of vulnerability was quickly masked behind a deathly glare. 'And she says it's your fault!'

Cal's blood boiled. 'What are you talking about?'

'Vi'Toria!'

'I only spoke to her once! I didn't do anything. She's the one who owes me an apology.'

'She's a Kisame, you idiot! You probably haven't even done it yet.'

'I—what?'

Cal turned Thorn's meaning over. The Kisame ancestors were the Elders of prosperity and time, for their clan's mental arts interacted with the past and future. Was Vi'Toria one of the rare few who could glimpse things to come?

'I can't explain something I haven't done yet!' Cal said, exasperated.

'Damon's going to be pissed when he learns you're the reason his peace treaties fell apart. Some emperor's apprentice you are.'

Thorn stomped away, clearly agitated. As he turned into the next corridor, he appeared to check and make sure no one was following him. Where was the princeling going without a military escort?

Cal narrowed his eyes.

'Go to bed after dinner. I won't be back tonight,' he said to Jaiyan, and reached for his military coat.

'I hate you!' Jaiyan snatched an empty inkpot and aimed to throw it. Cal shut the door and heard it shatter on the opposite side.

---

Thorn was incredibly easy to follow. Most people were, if you had nebula gates.

Cal waited until Thorn was out of sight, then drew his next oval for the furthest point. He stepped out and regained a clear view of Thorn: who purposefully trailed through the winding city alleys, as if to lose followers. He looked like a fool, constantly stopping to listen for footsteps—steps Cal never had to make.

Thorn entered an expensive-looking inn. Cal watched from outside as Thorn spoke to the innkeeper behind the bar. He was pointed upstairs via a quiet stairwell. Cal studied the windows above and counted across. Guessing the room, and judging the tiled roof to be sturdy, Cal drew and stepped onto the awning.

A breeze from the rooftops ruffled him, and he stooped down low. From here Cal could see the Ferryway bridge and the busy lower city. No one shouted nor pointed at him. Most people below seemed enamoured by the stalls and shop fronts, many of which were trading late with the influx of visitors to the capital.

Cal pressed his ear to the window hinge and was rewarded with the sound of muffled voices. He couldn't hear them all, but there was at least one older woman close to the window. Hidden by the shadows, he settled down to listen. What had the prince so rattled? What conversation was so important that it needed to occur in secret?

'Of course not. It has nothing to do with you,' the woman said. 'You've done well, Thorn. Do you wish to stay? My prince, you are welcome to leave the city with us. We would protect you from him.'

From *him*.

Cal picked at the loose thread of his red coat as he absorbed the words. It was easiest to think when his hands were busy.

'Vi'Toria cannot be sure. My daughter's journal entries are short and don't often tie together. We guess at the best path forwards with the information we have.'

*Vi'Toria*. The Kisame clan.

Something Rissa had said in the garden tugged at the back of Cal's mind. She had believed Damon's supporters would rally behind Cal instead of Thorn. She'd said it was because Thorn was the son of the former king, and Damon's supporters would choose new blood, if they had the option.

'The Assembly will dismantle itself. The Rytake, then the Hyate, and it's only a matter of time before he targets the Vissame. How many more clans must fall?'

But where did that leave the clans who opposed Damon's claim to the empire? Clans like the Kisame. Who did the emperor's enemies rally behind?

'Our plans have not changed. One king, one high priestess—the way it was when your parents ruled. Titles that are yours and Vi'Toria's by right.'

The loose thread from his coat snapped in Cal's fingers.

They rallied behind the prince, of course.

'We expect children from the union.'

Why would Damon take the son of the man he usurped to apprentice in the first place? In an attempt to appease the angry factions, no doubt. But by the sound of those words behind the window, Damon's plan had failed.

Cal studied the scarlet thread by the moonlight. He was invested now; he'd chosen his future. So what was to be done, now that he knew Thorn was a traitor?

Cal waited until Thorn was alone in the narrow alley. On his way back to the palace, the prince was being less careful now. He seemed confident he was not being followed.

He summoned a gate behind Thorn and did not hide his boot tread as he stepped out.

Thorn spun, nebula flaring.

Cal folded his arms, enjoying Thorn's flustered expression and raw hatred.

'You accuse me of destroying Damon's peace treaties,' Cal said. 'While *you* conspire with his enemies.'

Thorn sneered. 'If you ever believed I was loyal to him, then you're as stupid as the rest of them.'

'I haven't been using your correct title, have I?' Cal asked. '*Prince* Thorn. You call me an orphan, but that's what you are as well. Damon may have ordered the war on my kingdom—but he executed your parents himself!'

'I'm exactly where I need to be to make this empire mine someday.'

Cal could at least admire him for not denying it.

Thorn took a step forward. 'I'll return everything to how it was before the coup—to how things *should* be. But what's your excuse for following him? Did you just want to live in a palace? Damon is killing our people!'

*Our* people. Cal balled his fists.

'What do you know about the war? You've never lived in Dra'bah! What's stopping me from returning to the palace and telling Damon everything? He'll name me the heir before you've even made it back.'

Thorn tried to hit him. Cal slipped through a gate and emerged behind him.

But somehow Thorn predicted this. His second fist connected. It was a solid punch, cracking against Cal's jaw. He stumbled back and checked his teeth. Nothing was loose, but when he wiped his lip the back of his hand came away red.

'I'm glad you hit me,' Cal said. 'I'm also glad you attacked me in the gardens my first night. I wasn't going to accept Damon's offer. But every time you hit me, you tell me that you see me as a threat.' Cal's mist rose. 'You prove that you are afraid of me. You make me believe that I could actually be emperor someday.'

Thorn surged forward—as if aiming to knock him into the building's stone wall. With a flick of his wrist, Cal drew. A black oval appeared and Cal fell back through the space where the wall had just been. Thorn caught himself before tumbling after.

Emerging behind Thorn, Cal closed the gate and shoved—slamming his face into stone. Cal unsheathed his dagger, but was halted from doing anything more.

Six Kurakai warriors, their faces hidden behind black and white elderwood masks, sprung their ambush. Cal had not realised that *he'd* been followed.

He was struck with staves from multiple angles, and driven to the cobbles. His dagger was knocked from his grip. He pulsed—desperate to shield himself from the beating. He tried to draw, but a boot stomped his hand.

Arms protecting his head, he flared nebula. But his reserves were low. He'd hopped through too many gates this evening. He saw a glint of steel as a broadsword was slid from a sheath. Its wielder hovered nearby, waiting for Cal's defences to drain.

*Stars*, did they actually mean to kill him?

'I didn't need your help!' Thorn shouted. The staves driving into Cal lessened. Instead, knees and elbows now held him in place.

'We saw him attack,' a Kurakai said from behind her mask. 'This one does not deserve his place at the emperor's side.'

'What is your clan?' Thorn demanded.

Were these strangers to Thorn? Cal had assumed they were his Kisame allies.

'Danore,' the woman replied with a bow. 'Trust that we are friends. We only seek to replace this one with a worthy apprentice. He is the runt of an extinct clan, with blood so low he may as well be Numulai. No one will mourn his death.'

Danore. These Kurakai were Loretta's clan. It seemed her methods were a family affair. The woman gestured to her fellow assassin: the one with the broadsword.

'Kill him,' she commanded.

The palm pressed down, grinding Cal's hair beads painfully into the back of his skull. Cal fought to turn his head, and saw Thorn approach.

'I wasn't done here!' he said. 'I had this handled.'

'Best keep your hands clean, young master. Stand aside,' was the woman's response.

'You'd have me witness him be put down like some back-alley stray?' Thorn growled. 'The Coronation is supposed to be a fight! I earn nothing if I don't defeat him myself.'

Thorn held out his hand—waiting to be handed the sword. The Danore exchanged weighted glances.

The hilt was placed in Thorn's palm.

Dragged to his knees, Cal's head was shoved forwards and his neck exposed. He desperately tried to summon a gate—to imagine it materialise beneath him. Nothing happened. He needed his hands.

'Honourless bastard,' Thorn hissed, and Cal heard him lunge.

Warm blood dribbled down his neck, but it wasn't his. Cal twisted and saw Thorn's sword embedded into the chest of the Kurakai above him.

Thorn whirled and sliced at the Danore who'd relinquished the broadsword. The cut was deep. The man stumbled back, chest open. Cal scrambled free, retrieved his dagger from the ground, and drew a gate. Diving through, he buried the dagger into the woman's kidney.

Three dead or dying. The remaining three were defending now, and could not be taken by surprise. They were nebula-quick, and Cal tried to lash out—but the man protected his chest with mist and Cal's dagger point skittered uselessly off its surface.

An elbow took Cal in the temple. His vision blurred.

These were fully trained adult Kurakai. They wore their masks: the proud clan heirlooms of assassins. Like it or not, Cal and Thorn were only in the early days of their apprenticeship. They weren't going to win this fight.

Cal used his dwindling reserves to open a gate. Its pair was far away.

Thorn saw what he was doing. The prince was trapped, his back to a wall. He had a bloodied eye and all his weight was on one leg. The look he levelled at Cal could have scorched flesh: *Coward. Traitor.*

Cal escaped through the gate and into the void.

He emerged atop the snowy peak. Unable to feel the cold through drained limbs and hot adrenaline, Cal forced nebula-numbed fingers to dig for Ferocity. His insides constricted. It wasn't where he'd put it.

Cal shoved at another stone and saw the glint of rubies. Picking up the sword he felt its familiar song—it demanded to be used. His limbs ached, but he stretched his reserves to open a gate back. Hoping he'd successfully opened its pair, he stepped into the place between stars.

Blackness. A heartbeat longer than usual. Two.

His lungs burned—having never trusted himself to breathe inside the void. He reached and clawed to escape.

Gasping he stumbled into the alley. Thorn was on his knees, held between two Kurakai. They appeared to be arguing about what to do with him. Thorn's face was so swollen he wasn't certain if the prince had seen him return.

Cal stared at Ferocity, the priceless Regalia sword that answered to his blood. To the blood of his kingdom. To anyone who called Dra'bah home.

With the last of his reserves, Cal opened a hand-sized gate and passed Ferocity through. The sword clattered to the ground before Thorn, distracting the Kurakai who held him. Seizing the advantage, Thorn freed his hand and summoned the sword to his palm.

Then he started swinging. The man opposite Thorn never stood a chance within Ferocity's enormous reach. The blade penetrated his nebula defence and crunched through hip and spine. Thorn faced the next assassin on the follow-through, and struck with bludgeoning clangs against their weapon. Ferocity hungrily bit at its edge.

Cal's left hand fell limp, completely drained. Gritting his teeth, he retrieved from the woman's corpse a different type of sword: the single-edged kind, favoured by the Kurakai.

He darted forwards and slipped inside the final Danore's guard. Blade melding to Cal's style, the assassin was unprepared for his feint, and then the final blow. Cal raked the steel across his neck, exposing artery.

The man rasped, clutched at his throat, and died.

Cal stood over the mess, breathing hard. Seeing his tattered uniform, he could no longer tell the stains from the Dra'bish desert-red. He tried to shake his limp hand. It'd be a painful few days before movement returned.

Thorn too was fighting for breath as he took in the alley with a wide-eyed detachment. Like Cal, it appeared he'd seen this all before.

They stared at each other, their heaving breath visible in cool air. Pride wouldn't allow either of them to say it, but Cal would be dead without Thorn, and Thorn dead without him. Cal was grateful, and he saw in Thorn's forced shrug that he was as well.

Thorn turned Ferocity over and offered out the hilt. Cal traced his eyes over the rubies and for perhaps the hundredth time, wondered how many meals they were worth.

He decided it wasn't important, as it was the Swordarm that mattered, not the sword. Cal wouldn't become emperor if he continued to rely on shortcuts.

'Keep it,' he said. 'It doesn't suit my style.' He still held the Kurakai blade, so he slipped it through his belt.

Thorn examined Ferocity with a new appreciation. Cal hated how well the giant blade suited him.

Thorn grunted. 'Just as well. It is a weapon fit only for an emperor.'

'This is not me admitting that you're better,' Cal said, jabbing Thorn in the chest. 'I still intend to show Damon why I'll be his heir. And I'll do it without having you exiled for treason.'

Thorn was silent for a short moment. 'Damon doesn't respect the traditions. But you do,' Thorn said, then flushed. 'You better not shame me. We make each other stronger. That's the deal.' Thorn held out the flat of his palm. 'Apprentice-brother.'

Cal assessed the offered hand for hints of machinations, lies or hidden motives. All the things he'd come to expect from the palace. But for everything Thorn was—his arrogance and pettiness—he was genuine.

'Apprentice-brother,' Cal said, and placed his palm on top.

# About Precipice Fiction

We hope you have enjoyed this collection of short stories: some from realms completely different to our own, some not so far. These are only glimpses into wider works created by the authors, with full novel-length works incoming, so feel free to follow the individual authors for more info. We have worked very hard on this collection and are grateful to you, the reader, for going on this journey with us.

If you have enjoyed reading this collection and would like to support us, we would really appreciate you leaving a review on Amazon for us (or on Goodreads or StoryGraph if you prefer), as it allows other readers like you to find this book. If you'd like to read more of our work, you can download a free short story from www.precipicefiction.com/freestory.

Precipice Fiction hosts a weekly podcast called 'Prose and Cons' that you can find on any music streaming platform, where we discuss media and writing tips. You can also find us on Instagram, YouTube and TikTok: @precipicefiction.

Thanks again and we will see you soon!

*- Precipice Fiction*

Printed in Great Britain
by Amazon